JET NURSE

When Sheelagh's perfect future with Dr
Michael Kelman did not materialise, she took to
the skies as a jet nurse – and found a glamorous
pilot, Terry Fitzsimmons, who was only too
willing to take Michael's place. But were
Sheelagh's feet too firmly on the ground for her
to forget Michael – and *real* nursing – so easily?

JET NURSE

BY
MURIEL JANES

MILLS & BOON LIMITED
London . Sydney . Toronto

First published in Great Britain 1971
by Mills & Boon Limited, 15–16 Brook's Mews,
London W1Y 1LF

© Muriel Janes 1971
This edition 1980

Australian copyright 1980
Philippine copyright 1980

ISBN 0 263 73362 9

Set in 11 on 13½ pt Plantin

Made and printed in Great Britain by
Richard Clay (The Chaucer Press) Ltd.,
Bungay, Suffolk

CHAPTER ONE

DOCTOR MICHAEL KELMAN was the nicest thing that had ever happened to Sheelagh Landers. Tall and dark, he had the kind of personality that inevitably appeals to women; and because he was also conscientious and friendly he was one of the most popular doctors at the hospital. In addition to which, he was Irish! . . . He had enough Irish charm to make an impact even on the most resistant surfaces!

'He's a dream of a man, honey,' Sheelagh's room mate, Brenda Fitzsimmons, known to patients and staff alike as 'Fitzy', had said enviously on more than one occasion. 'If he so much as glanced in my direction for any other purpose than to request me to "Do this, Nurse," or "Do that, Nurse," I'd fall at his feet in instant capitulation. But he's so unlikely to do it I think my knees are safe!'

Fitzy was short and plump and homely, and despite her efforts to talk wisely and sound generally very worldly and with it, her appearance rendered vain her efforts. One look at Fitzy and one knew she wasn't fooling anyone, least of all herself.

That was one reason why Sheelagh liked her so much, and why she actually enjoyed sharing a room with her. With anyone else one could never be quite sure. . . . But with Fitzy one was always sure.

And as an English girl working in an American hospital it was necessary sometimes to be quite sure of someone. Not that everyone else was in league against her because of her nationality, but they did make fun of her accent and her slight English primness which was a part of her background—she came from Devon and on more than one occasion had been referred to as the Mayflower! Also her looks were strikingly English; she had naturally blonde, curly hair and an English rose complexion that, she felt vaguely, irritated some of her fellow nurses at times.

But none of these things irritated Fitzy, who made no bones about it that she frankly envied Sheelagh her looks.

Patients frequently paid tribute to them.

'You know, Nurse, you look so good I'd like to eat you,' a patient she was massaging after a minor operation for hernia told her as he lay looking—or rather, leering, she thought—up at her. He was a plump, middle-aged salesman, and she didn't particularly like him. He travelled in ladies' underwear and seemed to think he had an inside knowledge that revolted her.

'You'll do,' she replied briskly, as she finished him off rather quickly and dusted her hands that were covered with a fine film of zinc and boric acid starch powder.

It was close to quitting time, as Fitzy always called the nurses' shift periods. In less than a quarter of an hour the night staff would be coming on duty, leaving Sheelagh free to grab a meal, shower, and get herself dressed for her evening date with Michael. It was something she had been looking forward to ever since she opened her eyes that morning, and now she could barely wait to see him again.

In actual fact she hadn't long to wait before she actually cannoned into him in the corridor. He put out a hand to steady her, smiled down at her with all the Irish charm that was a part of his make-up looking out of his Irish eyes, and said softly:

'You in a hurry, Nurse? If you're not you should be a little more careful!'

Sheelagh felt as if her heart leapt up into her mouth, and from thence did a wild, convulsive contortion which promptly landed it right at his feet.

'Oh, Mike!' she breathed. 'I'm just going off duty.'

'That's no excuse for charging about in the corridors in a manner likely to prove harmful to

7

anyone heading in the opposite direction.' But there was a softness about the corners of his mouth that set her pulses fluttering, and he was gripping her shoulders with more warmth than actual force. 'Tell me,' he asked, while he made no attempt to release her, 'how's Petersen doing?'

Petersen was the man she had just been massaging, and she made a slight grimace.

'He's doing very nicely, thank you. I've just been attending to his bed-sores. But, quite frankly, I don't like him. . . . He talks too much about ladies' underwear!'

'He'll soon be on the road again, selling the stuff.' But he sounded rather thoughtful, as if the concerns of Mr Petersen were not really concerning him at all at that moment. And he eyed her rather more speculatively. 'I'm glad I've caught you, Sheelagh,' he told her, 'because I'm afraid I'm going to have to break our date for tonight! Wilky——' Wilky was Dr John Alexander Wilkins, Chief of Surgery—'has just telephoned, and he wants me to stay on. They've got an emergency . . . twelve cases up in Surgery now. He wants me to work through, at least until they clear the decks a little.' He straightened, removed a note-pad from his top pocket and studied it. 'This is the list for the Men's Ward—3-C,' nodding towards the swing doors next to which they were standing. 'I've got to inform the super. . . . Who is she, by the way?'

He lifted his expressive eyebrows and glanced down at Sheelagh.

'Northrupp—Anne Northrupp.' Sheelagh was trying to come to grips with her disappointment, and her voice sounded a trifle flat.

'Then she's going to be busy,' he predicted, 'because they've got ten of the twelve scheduled for 3-C.'

'She goes off duty in ten minutes,' Sheelagh reminded him. 'We all do.'

'Don't count on it, kid.' He had formed the habit of adopting Americanisms. 'I don't pretend to be familiar with the current strength of the nursing establishment in this hospital, and how many of you go off duty at any one time, but I do know we're in the midst of an emergency, and most of them will be staying the night. Now, better let me go on my way and rout out Miss Northrupp before she, too, slips away in the mistaken notion that she's free of all responsibility for the time being!'

Sheelagh had got over her disappointment, but because she couldn't resist detaining him a moment or so longer she asked:

'Why, what happened, Mike? It sounds as if there's been a riot, or something of the sort!'

'There was . . . or rather, two things happened at the same time that wouldn't normally do so. Hence the flap! A busload of tourists, coming back from seeing the Flag Day Celebrations in Golden Gate Park, collided with a semi-trailer on the corner of Turk and Van Ness Avenue, and a bunch of kids decided to have a gang war over in the Italian section of the town . . . Union Street, just down from Columbus.'

Sheelagh looked as shocked as she felt. She no longer bothered about missing an evening's date, and the born nurse in her banished the impressionable woman with absolute ruthlessness. She forgot that Mike was the man she was in love with—the man she hoped to marry one day!—and asked him further questions about the joint disasters. It was not the first time, living and working where she did, that violence had claimed her attention in such a way. Indeed, only a few days before she had been involved herself when a group out of Harlem had sought to settle their differences once and for all with another gang of Puerto Ricans.

The battle had been brief but bloody, and she knew she would never forget the sight of the terrible wounds these young people had inflicted on one another with their switch-blades.

It was part of the violent side of American life

that she was learning to take in her stride ...
nevertheless, with difficulty.

'I'm sorry about tonight, honey,' Mike said.
'But after all, there will be other nights, won't
there?'

'Of course.' But she smiled at him abstractedly.
'I'll come with you, Mike,' turning and passing
through the swing doors with him. 'Anne will
want someone to lend a hand getting things prepared.'

'Fine!' Mike patted her shoulder approvingly.
'That's my girl! ... The sort of thing I'd expect
from you, anyway.'

And she felt warmed and comforted despite her
disappointment, because she was, after all, his
girl, and he had the right to expect almost anything from her.

CHAPTER TWO

IT was very close to midnight when Sheelagh felt free to go off on her own. It really had been an emergency . . . quite one of the worst type.

She had no chance of another word with Mike, but Anne Northrupp had welcomed her offer of assistance and expressed herself gratefully on the subject.

Sheelagh, as she finally let herself into the room she shared with Fitzy, felt completely and utterly exhausted. It had been tough nursing, perhaps the worst kind after the labour ward, which she really hated. Post-operative nursing was crucial nursing. There were so many things that could go wrong after the patient had left the theatre, so many things for a highly experienced nurse who knew her job to do . . . pulse and temperature checks every half-hour or so, checks on respiration, on the blood-flow from the inverted bottles for the patients who had been ordered post-op transfusions. The thousand and one things that had to be done if the patient was to return to full health again.

'You look all in, honey,' Fitzy, who was lying on her bed with her reading lamp glowing softly about her head, observed sympathetically. She reached across and turned on Sheelagh's reading lamp for her. 'Get your feet up before your knees give way under you. I heard all about the emergency, of course. It was some emergency, wasn't it?'

Sheelagh nodded her head silently, and dropped down on the side of her bed.

Fitzy went on smoothing cold cream into her skin, and in the shine of the light about her head and face she really looked quite extraordinary, her features glimmering pallidly through the cold-cream mask.

'I thought there were too many volunteers already,' she offered, in explanation of the reason why she herself had not been among them. 'And, like too many cooks, they can sometimes get in one another's way. Besides, I see enough of that side as it is.'

Sheelagh smiled at her, watching her friend light and smoke a cigarette, and knowing full well that whatever Fitzy's faults she never shirked. And her ward drew some pretty tough characters, San Francisco being the chief seaport on the Pacific Coast. There was never any shortage of sea-going bums and derelicts, and other odds and ends of humanity washed up by the Pacific tides. Sometimes Sheelagh wondered whether they hadn't somehow slipped back in time, and were nursing some of the flotsam that had made the old Barbary Coast famous ... or infamous, according to the way you looked at it.

'No date tonight, huh?' Fitzy asked casually, reaching for the small glass ash-tray and balancing it on the bedclothes in front of her.

'No.' Sheelagh gazed wearily at her hands, that smelled strongly of antiseptic. 'Mike was up to his eyes—still is, as a matter of fact.'

'With Wilky?'

'Yes. I think they deserve a medal for what they did tonight.'

'Wilky's a very fine surgeon,' Fitzy remarked. 'I swear that man of yours worships the floor he walks on.'

'He is a very fine surgeon,' Sheelagh agreed, feeling herself suddenly stiffen, become almost defensive. 'Mike admires him tremendously.'

'You're telling *me*!' Fitzy tapped ash into the ash-tray and looked across at Sheelagh with suddenly shrewd eyes. 'I know this sounds crazy, but if I were you, honey, I'd be more than passingly jealous of Dr John Alexander Wilkins.'

Sheelagh smiled slightly and stretched out on the bed, cradling her arms beneath her head. She was too tired to answer, too tired to shower, all she wanted to do was relax and drift off into beautiful, restful, untroubled sleep.

Although she was staring up at the ceiling, Sheelagh sensed that Fitzy was watching her, was looking across at her closely. She sensed something else, too, that her room-mate had something on her chest that she wanted to get off it. And when Fitzy had something to say you had to listen, even if you'd drawn two duty stints straight and were out on your feet. Sheelagh sighed and turned her head so that she could look across at Fitzy. She had been right, she was staring at her—intently.

'I know something, honey,' she said when she saw Sheelagh looking at her, 'about your guy.'

'Mike?' Sheelagh jerked erect, sitting propped up on her hands, staring back at her friend. Like most plain girls, Fitzy went in for scandal, nothing nasty or vicious, certainly never anything harmful or cruel, but she did get a kick out of knowing what was doing in and around the hospital—a sort of sublimation of her natural romantic needs, which were frustrated into the next best thing, romantic gossip. And to Sheelagh's knowledge she had never been wrong yet in her snippets of scandal concerning hospital personnel. And now, it seemed, it was Mike's turn to have his name passed on through the hospital's grapevine.

'What do you mean?' Sheelagh asked, hearing

15

the tenseness in her own voice, annoyed that she had let it be so obvious, the fact that Fitzy's comment had reached her the way it had. 'What about Michael?'

'Wilky's going to offer him a residency.'

'He's going to do *what*!' Sheelagh's tension disappeared as quickly as it had come, and she did not attempt to keep her excitement from Fitzy.

'You heard me,' Fitzy grinned. 'It's what Mike wants, isn't it, to stay on here when his internship's over?'

'And he's going to do that? Gosh, he'll be beside himself when he gets to know about this!'

'I guess he does know, kid,' Fitzy's smile disappeared and she grew instantly contrite. 'Sorry, I guess I shouldn't have said that, at least not in that way. Me and my big mouth! I guess you hadn't heard, Mike hasn't told you about it, huh?'

'No.' Sheelagh looked away, into the shadows that filled the corner of the room next to her bed. 'No,' she said again, softly, too softly, 'he hasn't mentioned it to me.'

'Maybe he hasn't seen you, didn't get around to it.'

Sheelagh slowly turned to look at her friend, detecting the effort to patch things up, console her. She knew Fitzy hadn't *meant* to hurt her, it was just that she couldn't keep a secret, couldn't keep anything to herself. It all depended, she thought as she looked at Fitzy's white and shining face, on how long ago it happened. That was the deciding factor, determining whether or not she had cause to cry or laugh, excuse Michael, or begin to wonder and suspect him. She put the question into words.

'How long?' Fitzy echoed, shrugging and looking away, tapping ash from her cigarette with a stubby forefinger. 'I don't really know, hon, I guess a few days. Thelma Shand was second instrument nurse up in surgery last week. Remember old Mrs Davies, the one who was operated on for gall bladder and appendicitis at the same time? Well, Thelma overheard Wilky making the offer to Mike while they were closing.'

Last week! Why hadn't he mentioned it to her? Sheelagh's mind seemed to go whirling away from her, spinning at a tangent, so that she could barely concentrate on Fitzy's white, cold cream-shiny face, let alone her words. She could see her mouth moving, the lips opening and closing, but all sound was blanked out, as though the sound-track in her mind had ceased to function.

Last week! They'd seen each other a dozen times since then. Why hadn't he said something about it? It was great news, marvellous news for both of them, for it hadn't been easy trying to date on an intern's pay, and on most dates Sheelagh had insisted that she at least pay her share of either the meal or the price of her seat at the movies or theatre. And Mike *had* said, hadn't he, that once he got the money, was paid like a doctor and not like an unskilled handyman, they'd do something about the love that each felt for the other? Or was that all a dream, had it all been a figment of her imagination, a dream castle that she had somehow allowed herself to erect?

'Honey? Sheelagh?'

Sheelagh sensed rather than saw Fitzy hastily grind out her cigarette and swing her legs out of bed, hurry across to her. She perched herself on the edge of Sheelagh's bed, one hand tightly gripping Sheelagh's shoulder. 'Gee, kid, I'm sorry! Honey, are you okay?'

With an effort, Sheelagh forced herself to nod, then twist around and face her fellow-nurse. 'Yes, I'm fine!' she lied, smiling bravely, a smile that was no more than a grimace.

'Liar! You're all upset. So he didn't mention it!'

Sheelagh shook her head, not trusting herself to speak.

'Maybe . . .', Fitzy dropped her eyes to the cover of Sheelagh's bed, looking awkward and ill ease. 'Maybe he wanted it to be a surprise. Could be he's saving it until it's really definite, when he's been officially accepted by the board, by Kerensky.'

'I guess so,' Sheelagh smiled tightly and pushed herself up and away from Fitzy. Suddenly she wanted to be alone, wanted to think this thing out. Attempt to see it in some kind of perspective. And she knew she'd never do that while she was with Fitzy—now so anxious to patch up the damage her gossipy tongue had caused, to ease Sheelagh's mind. Heck, *nothing* could ease her mind! She didn't have a mind any more—only a pain-filled vacuum, a whirling, illogical mess that refused to accept the possibility that Dr Michael Kelman was *not* in love with her.

For how could any man, any young doctor, keep such wonderful news from the girl he loved, the girl he had promised to marry? If he wasn't prepared to share it with her, take her into his confidence then, quite obviously, he did not want Sheelagh to be a part of this new life, this life that Dr Wilkins had opened up for him by accepting him as a staff resident—surgery.

Sheelagh could scarcely remember leaving the nurses' quarters, could only vaguely recall hastily slipping into a dress and grabbing up her topcoat and bag before running from the room and Fitzy.

She had been driven by a mounting urge to be alone, compelled to be free of the hospital, the smell and look of which only further reminded her of Michael's secrecy. And she had run out through the hospital grounds, hailing the first cab she saw, riding in it until she felt she was far enough away from the massive bulk of the hospital building to feel free. And then she had called to the driver to stop and let her out, and only while she was fumbling in her purse for the fare money that she realised where she was, where the cab had taken her. Way downtown, on the waterfront—Jefferson Beach.

Now she was walking slowly through the fog that was so distinctive a feature of San Francisco, through the grey tendrils of mist that swept in from the bay, hiding the grim mass of Alcatraz—the old home of society's intractable male offenders, hiding, too, the famous Maritime Museum towards which she walked. This was Fisherman's Wharf, practically the closest one could come in the U.S. to a genuine Mediterranean port. The place they called the American Naples.

But Sheelagh was oblivious to the picture-postcard beauty of the spot, with the lights from the seafood restaurants and the countless waterfront bars reflected in the water. These challenged the shadows thrown by the clean, white-painted fishing boats that rode impatiently at their moorings, as though eager for the night to end so that they could once again feel the surge of the waves beneath their keels.

She did not hear the occasional wolf whistle that followed her, or the wisecrack or casual invitation thrown from some of the dark doorways that concealed either a drunk or some young sailor eager to have himself a ball.

What did it mean? That was the theme of her mental agony as she walked slowly along the waterfront. Was Michael through, were they through as a team? So this was the way it happened, Sheelagh mused, *bingo*, clear out of the blue. One minute you're tired and happy, thinking only of drifting off to sleep, the next your world's shattered, ruined, everything disintegrating as you reach out for it, as though by some crazy, slow-motion atomic explosion.

She stopped walking, leaning her elbows on the railing of one of the wharves, staring down into the heaving, constantly moving water. Although it was June, she wore a topcoat, a light tan coat with slash pockets, for San Francisco could be cold at night, no matter what the time of year, especially down close to the water.

Fog swirled around her, diffusing her with the

background of boats and boat sheds, insulating her from the rest of the city, so that she was in her own private little cocoon, locked away from humanity and reality, all alone with her misery.

Sheelagh suddenly shivered, as though someone had walked over her grave. She pulled her coat tight around her, jamming her hands deep down into the pockets, and for the first time she began to be afraid. What was she doing, anyway, walking the streets at this hour? This was the waterfront, a tough area, or tough enough for young girls alone.

Sheelagh glanced about her with worried eyes, then began walking quickly towards the lights of the restaurants and bars, her heels making a hard clacking sound that the fog did nothing to tone down or muffle.

She walked along the brightly-lit area, past the seafood eating houses, the delicious aromas drifting out to entice her so that, for the first time, Sheelagh realized how hungry she was, remembered that she had not eaten for more than twelve hours. Yet, despite her hunger, she knew that she could not eat a thing, not even one of the delicious dishes Fisherman's Wharf was famous for—crabmeat and prawns sauté with rice. Louis seafood salads, seafood *cioppino*—all the wonderful dishes she and Michael had sampled together, laughing when they compared the prices with what was left of Mike's intern pay and Sheelagh's nurse's money.

She felt a stab of pain then, a knife-like thrust in the region of her heart, and she knew, even as she swung towards the kerbside and flagged down a cab, hailing the driver in a voice that was little better than a choked cry, that it was only the first of many identical pains, that she would not be over her handsome Irish doctor for a very long time.

CHAPTER THREE

IT was close to dawn by the time Sheelagh got back to the nurses' quarters. The summer sun was already glinting golden-red in the windows of the houses atop the hills on which much of the city was built, while the dark canyons of the downtown streets were beginning to allow a little grey light to filter through, defying the right of the dying night to linger.

Fitzy came awake immediately as Sheelagh entered the room, started up in her bed, pushing her straight mousy-coloured hair back from her face, her dark blue eyes looking almost black in the faint grey light of dawn.

'And just where the heck have *you* been?' she demanded in a worried, angry voice. 'You've had me worried sick. If you hadn't come in by seven I was going to report it to the police, tell them you'd gone from here like a bat out of hell, in a very confused state of mind! They'd have gotten out an all points on you in nothing flat, and then everyone in the hospital would know what a kook I'm rooming with!'

She had been struggling out of bed as she

spoke, and now she stood in front of Sheelagh, both hands resting on Sheelagh's shoulders, looking at her with troubled eyes, her head on one side, her long loose hair falling in a cascade over her shoulder, her genuine expression of worried concern taking the sting from her words.

'Sheelagh, I'm so damned sorry, you'll never know just *how* sorry. I mean, heck, I wouldn't hurt you for worlds, you know that. I could kick myself for getting you all upset this way. I guess I didn't know just how overboard you were for that handsome hunk of Irishman.'

'Sure,' Sheelagh nodded, and somehow managed to dredge up a smile, knowing that her friend meant every word she had said, that what had happened had hurt her almost as much as it had hurt herself. 'I know, Fitzy. Stop worrying, feeling bad. I'm grateful to you, really ... it's better that I know. It gives me time to get used to things, prepare myself.'

'*Prepare* yourself!' Fitzy stepped back, staring at Sheelagh in open amazement. 'Kid, just what the heck do you mean? You sound like someone getting ready to do battle or something equally impulsive and stupid!'

Sheelagh smiled bitterly, shaking her head, biting her bottom lip, which had suddenly begun to tremble, straining to keep control of herself.

Do battle! Was that what she was thinking of doing? She was going to have to do *something*, that was for sure, but she knew she could never openly attack Michael, challenge him with this thing. She was not the type, rather, she was the type to run away from it all, attempt to shut it all out of her life, kill all the memories that had to do with Dr Michael Kelman.

Yes, that was it—run away, leave San Francisco, the hospital, maybe even nursing. Other girls had done it, she wouldn't be the first woman to drop her profession, get completely away from it, *do* something completely different. She realized suddenly that Fitzy was speaking.

'. . . so don't go rushing off and doing something you'll be sorry for. It's not the end of the world. Maybe Mike had a perfectly good reason for *not* telling you, like I said last night. Maybe he wants to be certain, get it made official. Maybe he just doesn't want to go raising your hopes only to have them come tumbling down when Kerensky and the board veto Wilky's proposal.'

'You're forgetting one small thing, Fitzy. Mike's Irish, real Irish. He could no more keep a thing like that to himself than he could turn away a sick person with no money to pay their hospital bill. You've heard about Irish impulsiveness—believe me it's a fact, and I'm one girl who should know.

'I guess so,' Fitzy smiled thinly, and made a vague gesture with her big hands. 'A girl whose name is Sheelagh, and with a sister named Oona, wouldn't be Scandinavian. On whose side is it, your mother's? Landers doesn't sound very Irish.'

'My mother's side,' Sheelagh nodded, 'she was an O'Claire before she married.'

'So you're convinced Michael's keeping this news to himself because he has some damned good reason for doing so.' Fitzy's voice brooked no argument. It was a statement of fact, not a real question.

Sheelagh nodded, silent for a moment while she forced herself to behave and appear normal, not allow her nerves to get the upper hand. Fitzy was being good and practical, she'd be the same.

'Yes,' she said at last, 'he hasn't told me because I'm not included in his plans. All right, so I've been fooling myself. I thought he loved me the way I love him, but I guess it never really is that way, is it, reciprocal? One always loves a little stronger, a little keener, a little deeper than the other. So he was lying when he used to talk about how good it would be when he was through his internship, was making some *real* money . . . I guess a guy has to talk about *something* when he takes his girl out. It won't kill me.' She managed

27

a sickly smile that was closer to being a grimace. 'I'm not the first girl to get too ambitious, get carried away on her own little ship of dreams.'

'I guess not,' Fitzy agreed, moving back and sitting on her bed, 'and you surely won't be the last. Okay, so let's forget it, huh? I've opened my big mouth, but as you say, maybe it was for the best, for it's better to know what's going on than to have it all suddenly thrown in your face like a dish of ice-water.'

Later that day, on duty in the ward, Fitzy's simile came back to Sheelagh. *A dish of ice-water in the face*. That's what it had been like, anyway, so how much worse would it have been if she'd been allowed to live in her fool's paradise a little longer?

The new cases that had come down from Emergency were already settling in, although two of the youths who had been injured in the gang rumble were on the danger list, their prospects uncertain. Both had suffered abdominal wounds, the knives penetrating through the abdominal wall and into the intestines. It was very much on the cards that they wouldn't make it.

Anne Northrupp beckoned to Sheelagh as she stood looking down at one of the youths, coming up on silent feet alongside the bed until her movement, the white blur of her, caught Shee-

28

lagh's eye, causing her to glance up at the ward super. Obediently she followed the older woman as she led the way back to her desk in the centre of the long ward.

'Sit down, Sheelagh.' She pointed to the spare chair opposite her own by the busy-looking desk, cluttered up with the report book, doctors' medicinal prescriptions for their respective patients, file cards, the inevitable white med. charts. 'Mind if I'm frank?' she asked when they were both settled.

'Frank?' Sheelagh frowned, wondering what was coming. Anne Northrupp was one of the most popular women in the hospital, it was unusual for her to take this sort of line. She usually left the lectures to Corinne Huntley. 'No, of course not!'

'What is it, Sheelagh, aren't you feeling well? Tell me if you're not and we can get a relief down. But, honey, you're honestly just not with us this morning!'

It was then that Fitzy's ice-water remark came back to Sheelagh. Anne Northrupp was as good as suggesting she had been walking around in a daze. Well, maybe she was in a trance—a shock-induced one, the sort of zombie-like state that afflicts people who *have* had a dish of ice-water flung at them.

'Sorry,' Sheelagh somehow managed a quick, apologetic smile. 'I . . . I had rather a bad night.'

'It's more than tiredness, Sheelagh,' Anne Northrupp's wise, knowledgeable eyes searched Sheelagh's face, her voice, stern with conviction, challenged Sheelagh to deny the statement. 'I'm sorry, but I really think I should ask you to go off duty, so you can go get a little rest.'

'Go off duty!' Sheelagh's voice echoed her shocked amazement. Just how stupidly had she been behaving, anyway? She *really* must have been acting oddly for someone like Anne Northrupp to take such an extreme measure. It was the first time she'd heard of a senior ordering a nurse from a ward, and Sheelagh could, she knew, be grateful that it happened to be Anne Northrupp, because with Anne she knew it would go no further. Anne would cover for her, would write it up as being due to sudden sickness, something common and general, like maybe gastritis, likely to afflict anybody at any time.

'I'm sorry,' Anne's expression was kindly and sincere, and, looking at her, Sheelagh knew that she hated having to do it, hated having to send her back to Quarters. 'But we've got some pretty sick people here, Sheelagh, especially those two boys I saw you gazing at just now. They need meticulous nursing if they're to pull through, and

30

even then it'll be touch and go. We just can't afford to have somebody around who isn't one hundred per cent efficient, and I'm sure you'll be the first to agree on that.'

Sheelagh nodded silently, knowing that Anne was only speaking the absolute truth, that an inefficient nurse automatically jeopardized the lives of her patients, the men, women and children in her care.

'Just how bad was I?' she asked in a voice scarcely louder than a whisper. 'Did I do anything wrong? Please, Anne, tell me . . . I want to know!'

The older woman glanced down at her desk, her cheeks colouring with sudden embarrassment, as though she was loath to tell Sheelagh the facts, the reason for her having made her decision. 'You almost gave Mr Pascoli *Tinctura Belladonnae* instead of *Tinctura Digitalis*,' she said finally, looking up at Sheelagh apologetically. 'I saw it, luckily. Remember I sent you to check Mr Marlowe's pulse and temp., said I'd take care of Mr Pascoli?'

Sheelagh nodded silently, feeling her face grow stiff and rigid, drained of blood, feeling, too, the sudden tight contractions that are the first, the immediate symptoms of shock or fear. The two drugs didn't even look alike. *Belladonnae* was clear and green in colour and was given to gastric

31

ulcer patients before meals to diminish the secretion of acid, while *Tinctura Digitalis* was a dark brown liquid and was used as a heart stimulant.

Nobody would have died because of the mistake—a mistake that Sheelagh could not, even now, remember having made, but that wasn't the point. The point was, as Anne Northrupp had gently but firmly emphasized, there were many very bad cases in the ward, patients requiring the most careful and expert nursing. People who just might not make it if they depended upon a nurse so mixed-up in her own emotional affairs that she was virtually useless, worse yet, who posed a definite threat to their chances of recovery.

Anne Northrupp went on: 'That was one instance. The other, the one that forced me to have this little talk with you, Sheelagh, was when I called you three times and you didn't even hear me, didn't seem to be aware of my existence . . . or your own, for that matter!'

Sheelagh just sat there helplessly, staring into the kindly features of the senior nurse. What was there to say? What *could* she say? That she didn't remember the two incidents? That she hadn't meant to get the two drugs mixed?

'Is there something wrong, Sheelagh?' Anne leaned forward, frowning with worry, anxious to help. 'You don't have to tell me if you don't want to, but if there's anything I can do, it goes without saying you have only to ask.'

'It ... it ...' Sheelagh bit her lip, feeling the hotness behind her eyes that always precipitates the actual tears. She wanted desperately to tell someone about Michael and herself, to get some of the unbearable pain out of her system, ease the immense weight that seemed to be pressing down upon her chest. She knew that talking about it was the one way of achieving this, of hastening the slower and only real medicine—the passing of time.

'I guess,' she said at last, her voice taut, quivering with the emotional tension that gripped her, 'it's just personal, Anne, something that I'll have to work out for myself. But thanks a million for offering to help, you'll never know just how much I appreciate that!'

'Well, I won't pry.' Anne placed the palms of both hands flat on the top of the desk, a gesture that suggested their little talk was over. 'But I will say this, I've been a nurse a long time now, and I've seen—and known—what happens to women when a certain dream doesn't materialise. It passes, Sheelagh, we get over it ... we get over everything in time, even though we don't always feel we will, can't believe, possibly accept the fact that life is possible *without* a certain person to share it with.'

Sheelagh nodded, smiling through the tears that now filled her eyes, that coursed unheeded down her cheeks, dripping down on to the starched whiteness of her uniform. 'Thank you,' she managed to get out . . . 'so very, very much!'

And then she fled the ward, oblivious to the curious stares of the patients as she ran between the two rows of beds towards the swing doors. The doors that now seemed to symbolize safety and warmth and the privacy she craved. The doors in which—what now seemed a million years ago—she had crashed headlong into Dr Michael Kelman.

CHAPTER FOUR

HE looked tired and very serious, the usual good humour gone from his face, his eyes. Even his stance was different, his shoulders hunched over, his hands deep-thrust in the pockets of his white coat.

News of his call had reached Sheelagh less than a half-hour after she had gone to her room. A tapping on the door was followed by the voice of another nurse calling that she was wanted on the phone. It had been Michael, saying that he wanted to talk to her urgently. Could she meet him in the entrance to Wing B?

She hadn't wanted to. All Sheelagh had felt like doing when she finally reached the haven of her room was bury her face in the pillows and sob her heart out. But there had been something about Michael's voice, the deepness that came close to being downright sombre, that had filled Sheelagh with a sense of urgency, so that she knew she was powerless to refuse him, that she just simply *had* to go. She was like a puppet obeying the jerking of its strings, was a creature lacking any mind of its own, any individual volition.

'Hello, Michael!'

He turned quickly when he heard her voice, spinning around in fast nervous—or was it guilty?—reflex. 'Honey! Thanks for coming, I was worried that perhaps you wouldn't.'

'You want to talk here?' Sheelagh glanced around her as she spoke, a glance that took in the busy entrance foyer in which they stood.

'No, outside,' he touched her arm and pointed to the plate-glass doors, 'if that's okay with you.'

Outside, he led her down the side of the wing to a relatively quiet spot opposite the doctors' parking lot. The sun was very hot, and the bricks were warm to her back as Sheelagh leaned against the wall waiting for him to speak, looking up into his tense and troubled face with a tranquillity that amazed her. It was as though she had cried her way clear through her original emotional upset, was enjoying the calm that follows any storm, or was this merely the 'eye' of a hurricane?

'Your room-mate, Fitzy, came to see me,' he said in a slow, careful manner, as though he was selecting each word separately before uttering it aloud. 'She told me what happened.'

'Oh!'

Sheelagh just stared at him. *Damn Fitzy! Hadn't she done enough?* she thought angrily. Most probably this was only her way of squaring off, an attempt to undo the damage her careless, thoughtless gossip had done, but why did she have to go to Mike Kelman? Hadn't she been able to guess at the embarrassment such an action would cause everyone concerned?

'I guess,' Michael went on, losing a little of his original forcefulness, beginning to look awkward and ill at ease—as Fitzy had done, as Anne Northrupp had done, 'that we would have had to talk this thing out eventually. Maybe it's better that it's out, Sheelagh, that you know about the residency.'

'Why, Michael?' Sheelagh asked, fixing him with a long, hard stare, finding pleasure in seeing him virtually squirm beneath it. 'If you don't want to be burdened with a wife just say so. I'm not made of some high-quality glass or priceless porcelain. I won't shatter into a million pieces. Just act like a man and tell me straight out, to my face—now, that you want to forget the promises you made, the things we used to talk about. That you've decided you want to do this alone, feel free to throw yourself into your work without the complicated demands that all women make upon their husbands, the normal and natural demands of marriage!'

It was quite a speech, and the intensity of it rather shocked and scared Sheelagh. She'd *really* opened up, loosed off a broadside. Well, now it was up to him, the ball was in his court. Yes or no, a good clear-cut and practical answer to things, that was the best, the only way.

He took his time. He let her sweat, or so it seemed to Sheelagh as she watched him look at his shoes, at the row of parked cars in the lot in front of them, down towards the entrance, finally up into the air, as though he were checking the guttering. Anywhere, in fact, but at her.

'How do I say it?' he shrugged, a helpless sort of gesture, finally managing to spare Sheelagh a sideways glance before continuing his study of the guttering along the east side of B Wing. 'I love you, you know that, but I've been having a few long talks with Wilky, Kerensky, too.'

'And they've persuaded you to forgo marriage for a while, is that it?'

'Well, in a way, I guess they did sort of get around to mentioning the fact, yes.' He nodded jerkily and looked down into Sheelagh's face, his honest, normally fun-loving hazel eyes very serious as they finally met her level stare.

'Nice of them! I must remember to mention to their wives how much they admire and enjoy the happy and sacred state of matrimony at the next Christmas or New Year's party!'

'Honey,' he made a weary gesture and a frown

38

hooked itself down over his forehead, narrowing his eyes, 'they were trying to help me, were trying to pass on the benefit of their own personal experience. They were both interns once, you know, they know what it's like, the problems, the tremendous challenge surgery is ... if a doctor really wants to make a success of his career.'

'No woman to hamper him, huh? No emotional strings, no obligations of a personal nature like a wife who loves and admires her doctor husband, like maybe a kid or two, a son or a daughter to think about, worry over!'

Sheelagh was, she knew, beginning to get hysterical. She fought the urge, clenching her hands up into fists, pressing her back against the hot bricks of the wall. *This wasn't the way*. Be practical, be sensible, be logical, *that* was the way. But it was a little difficult to achieve that desired state when one's world, all of one's dreams, were dissolving around one, tinkling down in a billion pieces, like cruel snow. Michael was saying:

'Sheelagh darling, try to understand, try to see it my way—our way. Both Wilky and Kerensky have been married twice, I don't know if you knew that, but it's a fact. Both married when they were interns, when they worked together in New York, at the Vanderbilt.'

'And the current divorce rate for America is

one in every three marriages,' Sheelagh cut in, her voice, even to her own ears, beginning to sound shrill. 'And that naturally includes physicians and surgeons!'

'Honey,' Michael passed a tired hand over his face, shaking his head wearily, his voice slow, patient, exactly the manner a doctor would adopt with an hysterical woman patient he happened to be rather fond of. 'It's not giving things a chance, the demands are too great, from both sides, both directions. Marriage, in its first few months, is a very delicate state of affairs. More marriages founder in the first year, especially with very young couples, than any of us really realize, bother to think about. It demands so much from the individual, there's so much to cut away from one's own personality if it's to match up in any sort of harmony with one's partner.'

'What they call the adjustment period, I believe,' Sheelagh said sarcastically, suddenly wanting to hurt him, to hit back, cause Michael the sort of hurt his attitude had made her suffer.

'Okay,' he snapped back, his eyes lighting with sudden anger, 'so you know about it, but that doesn't detract from the fact that it's a problem everyone who enters marriage has to face. With me, with us—at this time, there'd be other demands, as great, if not greater, than the emotional, the personal ones.'

'Turning yourself into a great doctor, you mean.' Sheelagh could not keep the sarcasm from her voice, somehow, even though she was already ashamed of having allowed herself the dubious pleasure of purposely causing him pain.

'It's not easy,' Michael said stiffly, coming suddenly erect, so that, looking at him, Sheelagh could all but see the tension and anger that now filled him, as though she had X-ray-like access into his mind. 'And as a nurse you should be the first to realize and appreciate the fact! Or don't you *want* to even try and see things my way any more? Hell, I'm doing this for us, can't you see that? Because I don't want my marriage to go sour the way it did with Wilky and our medical superintendent—Alex Kerensky. When I marry I want it to be you, Sheelagh, and I want it to last—for ever. I don't want to be numbered in that tragic "third" of the population who find they've made a mistake with their lives and so walk out on their vows, their promises, in most cases on happiness. Because you can't tell me that a very damned big percentage of people who get themselves divorced don't later regret it!'

Sheelagh closed her eyes and hugged her arms around herself. Which way did she go? What should she believe? It made sense, and any girl would be thrilled beyond measure to hear her man say the sort of things Michael just had, show such a sense of value and appreciation towards life and love.

But surely, and this was seeing it purely from her own, from the woman's side, a man who loved somebody as much as Mike claimed to love her, would have enough faith in that love, in Sheelagh as a person, to risk the dangers inherent in an early marriage. Because if their mutual love wasn't strong enough and deep enough to carry them safely through those early emotional rapids, it wasn't strong enough to bind them together for eternity.

So which way did she go? Which way *should* they go? Was Michael, with his cautious approach to marriage, right, or was her own strictly impulsive desire to marry first and to hell with the consequences the correct answer to the problem? Because who, after all, was to say Michael was right, that Wilky was right, that Kerensky had been right? Where was the percentage in worrying about something that might never happen?

Sheelagh, her mind made up, slowly opened her eyes, looked up into the face of the man she loved, searching it, examining it closely, feature by feature. A shiver passed through her, and she hugged her arms even tighter around herself.

'So your mind's made up, you want a respite, a breathing spell. You want to work as a resident for a while before we start setting the date and worrying about who to invite and who to leave out of the list of invitations, is that it, Michael?'

'You don't agree with it, do you?' he asked slowly, again seeming to weigh his words before speaking them aloud. 'You feel let down, cheated.'

'Oh, no, I'm delirious at the idea!' Sheelagh gave a high, nervous laugh, a sound so shrill and naked and somehow horrible that it made her want to cringe. *Watch it!* her common sense screamed at her, *you'll ruin everything if you lose control, allow yourself to come apart!* 'It'll give me five years in which to plan my trousseau!'

'I guess I should have told you before,' he went on, his light brown eyes filled with a mixture of sadness and self-recrimination. 'I guess I just couldn't find the courage to bring it up, that's all.'

And that was how they parted. Neither spoke again—there was no need for words. Looking at one another, looking deep into one another's eyes, both Sheelagh and Michael knew that this was it, that their views had placed them on opposite sides of the fence. They were like the opposite poles of a magnet now—instead of attracting one another they were repelling.

Fitzy came in just as Sheelagh was completing her packing. A lot had happened. First, Sheelagh had gone to see Corinne Huntley, the staff super, and handed in her resignation from the hospital—to take effect immediately. As expected, the most-hated super in the entire hospital had reacted badly towards both the immediacy of the resignation and to Sheelagh. She virtually abused her for letting the hospital, herself, in fact the nursing profession down by such behaviour. Sheelagh, who had been expecting just such a storm, took it in her stride, for the break-up with Michael had left her insulated against anything else, any other sensations, especially from personalities like Nurse Huntley's.

There was no home for her to go to, for both Sheelagh's parents were dead—her father in an accident at work—he had been a truck driver, a 'wildcatter' or 'gypsy', a man owning his own truck and anxious to pay it off in the quickest possible time by working the longest possible hours. He had fallen asleep at the wheel and had been killed instantly when the truck had run off the highway and overturned into a culvert. Her mother had died of cancer less than a year after Sheelagh had begun nursing, was still a student.

So there were only the two of them, Oona, the eldest by nearly five years and married to a clerk in a large New York department store who would never be anything other than a clerk in a department store, and Sheelagh. And Sheelagh, well aware of her sister's plight, the sort of dull, penny-pinching existence she eked out, trying to bring up her three children right in a neighbourhood that could boast of one of the highest rates of juvenile delinquency in New York, had no desire to go to Oona with her troubles.

And so she had begun packing, not knowing where she would be going, having no plans other than the immediate one—to get out of San Francisco, get as far away from the hospital and Michael Kelman as possible.

'I heard about it,' Fitzy closed the door and leaned against the wall, pointing to the open suitcase on Sheelagh's bed, the open drawers, the tumble and jumble of odds and ends still to be packed away. 'I couldn't get away, we had three patients coming down from surgery and two of the students didn't show up. I haven't had time to breathe all day.'

Sheelagh nodded, sinking down into the one tiny cane armchair the room boasted. News that

45

she had resigned would, she knew, have flashed all over the hospital minutes after she had left Corinne Huntley's office. It was like a small town, with everyone knowing what everybody else was doing. It would be nice to become a no-nentity again, lose oneself—as a stranger—in some other city.

'I guess,' Fitzy's mouth grew into a small sour line as she perched on the foot of Sheelagh's bed, automatically reaching out to the bedside table they both shared for cigarettes and lighter, 'you didn't pay much attention to what I said about not rushing off and doing something foolish, something you'll be sorry for.'

'I guess maybe I didn't,' Sheelagh smiled briefly, watching as her friend lit a cigarette and inhaled deeply, gratefully, as though it was something she'd been craving for hours. She was going to miss Fitzy, she knew, miss her a lot, for they had grown very close during the time they'd shared the room together.

'What happened exactly?' she asked, looking across at Sheelagh, her eyes squinting from the smoke as she lazily exhaled, allowed the smoke to dribble slowly from her nostrils, out from between her parted lips. 'Big row with Mike? I hoped that if he saw you, you two would straighten things out. Looks like I went and did it again, huh?'

'I'm afraid so,' Sheelagh admitted, smiling again. Despite the fact that she had been more than passingly angry at her for having taken the liberty of going to see Michael, telling him everything that had happened, now that she had so honestly and openly confessed to the fact of having again botched things, Sheelagh found it impossible to be anything else but sorry for her pathetically plain, well-meaning room-mate.

'But don't worry about it,' she went on, trying to sound light and casual about the whole thing. 'I know you were filled with nothing but good intentions when you hunted him out.'

'That's for sure!' Fitzy replied emphatically, her expression saying how much she appreciated the attitude Sheelagh was taking, how glad she was that they weren't having a scene. 'Anyway,' she waved her hand around the room, indicating once again the open suitcase, the general mess that always goes with packing, 'I won't try and talk you out of this, because I think I've known you long enough to know when your mind's made up about something. I'll content myself with just one question. Just where the hell are you going?'

'That's really the sixty-four-thousand-dollar one, isn't it?' Sheelagh admitted. 'I don't know, I haven't made any definite plans. All I want to do is get away from 'Frisco.'

' 'Frisco or Mike?'

'Both, I guess.'

Fitzy was silent for a minute, smoking and looking at Sheelagh thoughtfully, as though making up her mind to something. Then she went across to her dressing table and from the top drawer pulled out a brown leather photograph album. She opened it and then handed it to Sheelagh. Sheelagh looked at the six-by-eight photograph that completely filled the page. It showed a blond man of about twenty-five or so, with a wide infectious grin, what looked to be twinkling blue eyes, and the sort of features one usually associated with a Broadway actor. He was dressed in some kind of uniform, but what it was Sheelagh couldn't be sure.

'Nice,' she smiled, handing the album back, wondering just what the photograph of a blond-headed glamour boy had to do with her at this particular stage of things, 'anyone we know?'

'My brother.'

Sheelagh nearly fell out of her chair in surprise. Fitzy, recognising her amazement, nodded and grinned wryly. 'No family resemblance, is there? Just one of those things, those lousy, unfair quirks of Dame Nature that makes girls like me become either alcoholics, D.A.s, or just plain old-fashioned neurotics. The same parents, same grandparents, and Terry looks like something out of a movie while I look the way you see me now ... a has-been before I'm twenty-five. Maybe that's why I don't talk very much about him, I guess it's that I'm just too damned jealous and mad.'

Sheelagh wanted to say something, wanted to comfort her in some way, but she knew there was nothing she could do or say, nothing anybody could do or say, that would help Brenda Fitzsimmons.

She would always be plump, plain Fitzy, the girl who just went to help make up the number, to whom nothing exciting ever happened or was ever likely to happen. Sheelagh, looking up at her friend, didn't blame her in the least for feeling sore. As Fitzy had said, Dame Nature had pulled a pretty low-down trick on the Fitzsimmons family.

'Anyway,' Fitzy pulled herself together and smiled a wide smile, 'now you know. I have a *very* good-looking brother. I told you about him because I think maybe he'll be able to help you, in fact when he sees you I'm damned certain he'll help you.'

'Help me?' Sheelagh lifted her brows, remembered the vague suggestion of a uniform, wondering just what it was that Terry Fitzsimmons did that he could help a nurse in distress.

'He flies,' Fitzy explained, taking a long pull at her cigarette and resuming her seat on the foot of Sheelagh's bed. 'He's one of the turbo-jet boys, which to hear Terry talk is very much the élite in his particular racket.'

'A pilot?' Like most girls, Sheelagh was always mildly thrilled when she met up with, or talked about, the flying fraternity, something that, especially to a hard-working nurse, seemed very much a glamour profession.

'Co-pilot,' Fitzy nodded, 'what they call a First Officer, which means he wears two rings on his sleeve. He's flying Boeing 707s, and he loves it.'

'I bet he really sees the world,' Sheelagh said, knowing a tinge of envy for the handsome young pilot, unconsciously comparing his life to her own comparatively narrow existence. When she'd flown across to New York she'd felt as though she were going off on some kind of an expedition, was an intrepid explorer. How must it feel, she wondered, to take off every week for other countries? England, France, South America, Australia, Africa? And Fitzy had suggested that he might be able to help her! Sheelagh knew a thrill of anticipation, moved forward until she was perched on the edge of her chair, anxious not to miss a single word Fitzy said.

'Right now he's doing a course, in Washington

I think, that's the head office for the line he works for. Maybe if I give him a ring he'll get something organized—they get free air travel, of course, so it'd be no problem to get him to fly across, or if I talk hard enough he might pull a few strings and get you booked for a free flight. That would at least fulfil most of your hopes, would get you away from San Francisco.'

'Fitzy,' Sheelagh could scarcely believe the wonderful, the fantastically surprising news that had, quite literally, burst clear out of the blue, 'you'd really do that, go to so much trouble? What if he's too busy? You said he was doing a course, so he can't just drop everything, forget his studies, and help a perfect stranger!'

'You're not a stranger, kiddo,' Fitzy grinned, leaning across and grinding out her cigarette in the ash-tray. 'You're my friend. Maybe I can't exert much noticeable influence on strange males, but although I say so myself I can usually get Terry to jump through a few hoops when I want him to. So you just relax, just leave it all to your old Aunty Fitzy! There's only one way out of this mess you seem to have landed yourself in ... or maybe I landed you in it, I'm not quite sure. And that's to fly you out. And, like I say, it just so happens that I have a brother flying the jets!'

CHAPTER FIVE

AND that was the way it was to go—at jet speed.
Almost before Sheelagh knew it she had talked to
Fitzy's brother in Washington, telling him about
her nursing experience, promising that yes, she
was a fully qualified R.N.—this in answer to his
first and only real question—and saying she was
free to catch a plane out of 'Frisco any time.

Fitzy came to see her off, along with Anne
Northrupp and one or two of the other nurses
who had gone through at the same time as herself, and who had known her since her student
days. There was a certain amount of emotion
about the send-off because they were all firm
friends, and the fact that Sheelagh was English
had never made any real difference to the quality
of the ties they forged. They were years Sheelagh
knew she would never forget, years she would
want to recall often in after days, when, perhaps,
she was married—to someone very different from
Michael (although at this painful stage of her existence there was only one man in her life, and
that was Michael!)—with children and grand-
children of her own, to whom she could relate her

experiences. The days that would always be known as her hospital days.

At the very last moment she saw Fitzy particularly through an actual film of emotion that was absurdly close to tears, and then the jet was lifting from the huge international airport, boosted up at an alarming angle, its shiny nose pointing for the sky, and from the hospital. Fitzy, her friends and Dr Michael Kelman were all left behind, and Sheelagh was being launched into what promised to be the most exciting phase of her young life. . . .

But before this conclusion to her hospital days there was no escaping a final farewell with Michael. Sheelagh would have infinitely preferred to spare herself this ordeal, not because she was afraid it might weaken her resolution but because any contact with Michael—even in thought—at this present stage was like opening an old but still raw wound, which could cause her infinite pain.

However, Michael had become so much a part of her life that she could not just shake him off or discard him like an old garment. According to his lights he had done nothing in the least outrageous, and even if she had planned to slip away without goodbye he saw to it that she didn't.

Once her resignation had been handed in and

accepted, her trip to Washington finalized, the hospital grapevine saw to it that he got to know of her intentions.

She had been packing hard in preparation for leaving when word reached her that he was waiting for her in the doctors' parking lot. Fitzy, who was there when his request to have a word with her was delivered, looked hard at her as she slammed down the lid of a suitcase.

'You must see him, Sheelagh,' she said.

Sheelagh stared back at her.

'Why?'

'Because you owe it to him. Because he hasn't done anything anti-social.'

'He's ruined my life!'

'Rubbish! You're planning to have a good time in the skies. Remember?'

'I haven't even been taken on by the airline yet.'

'No, but you will be. . . . You'll see!'

Sheelagh decided she had no option but to grant Michael his last request. After all, what did it matter . . .? After today she and Michael would be pursuing different roads, and the sooner he realized it the better.

Mentally licking her lips, she looked forward to the moment when by some lucky break his pride could be hurt, even his dignity upset. No doubt he had been thinking that while not requiring to eat his cake at the moment he could keep it in reserve for later on ... perhaps five years hence! It might even be ten years if it took him that length of time to climb to a position from which elevation he would feel justified in taking such an important step as marriage—with Wilky's permission, of course!

Fitzy watched her go, chin up and with lips set tightly. She felt a certain sympathy for Dr Michael Kelman as she did so.

But Michael, despite the rumours he had heard, did not look particularly apprehensive.

He was waiting in the parking lot when Sheelagh joined him. She had already discarded her uniform and was wearing a trim civilian outfit, one in which she proposed to journey to Washington.

'Hullo, honey!' Michael greeted her.

Sheelagh returned stiffly:

'Hullo, Michael!'

There was a faintly whimsical expression on his face; the mere suggestion that he was prepared to go a long way to humour her in his exceptionally attractive eyes.

'You're looking pretty good, darling,' he told her. 'Not thinking of going anywhere special, are you?'

'To Washington,' she answered.

A shadow crept across his face.

'I heard you had some plans,' he admitted, 'but I felt certain you'd tell me all about them before you set off.'

'Why?' she demanded, annoyed because he had called her darling as if everything was still the same between them.

He shrugged his shoulders slightly.

'No particular reason, except that you and I usually tell one another our plans.'

This was an unwise observation on his part, and she pounced upon it instantly.

'Except the one important occasion when you started climbing the ladder and didn't seem to think it could be of any possible interest to me! Although I understand now that although you probably thought it might interest me you didn't consider that it actually concerned me!'

'Now look here, Sheelagh . . .' He advanced towards her, but she retreated until she came up against the gleaming near-side door of one of the visiting consultants' cars. Michael's Irish eyes betrayed sudden annoyance.

'You know perfectly well that everything I do concerns you, and when I told you that I wanted time to establish myself before making myself responsible for the support of a wife and family I didn't mean that you and I were going to part. I took it for granted that you would understand and be prepared to go on as we are for a year or two longer ... just so that we could be secure when we did marry. And it isn't as if you weren't happy in your job, and that we didn't have ample opportunities to see one another. . . .'

'Too many opportunities, no doubt you think,' she remarked to him sarcastically.

He looked as if she had delivered a smart slap across his face.

'Sheelagh, you're merely being spiteful!'

'On the contrary,' she assured him, 'I've suddenly become a realist, and realists always see things in a different way. For years now I've been tagging along in your shadow—the august shadow of a future Resident!—but not any longer. I haven't been all that happy in my job, all that dedicated!

'Women age more quickly than men, and they like to settle down, to have things clear and cut and dried. For all I know two, or even three, four or five years from now, you might still be shrinking from linking your life with mine! Someone might offer you a prize plum of a job that would make it highly undesirable you should have such a thing as a wife, and as your patient and long-suffering fiancée I would have to accept it that another long waiting period *must* lie ahead of us. And I don't suppose you'd be any more sympathetic than you are now . . . because for one reason you'd probably be getting a little tired of me in any case, and for another the world is full of women eager to snaffle a rising young doctor as a husband, and the knowledge that you were in a kind of way tied to me might make you pretty bitter.'

'What utter nonsense!' he exploded.

'It isn't nonsense, and as a matter of fact it's indisputable common sense! Poor little Sheelagh, who was always waiting and was prepared to go on waiting for another hundred years if necessary for her man! Only it just so happens that I'm not prepared to wait, and although it may come as a bit of a shock to you since you seem to have rather a generously inflated ego the only words I have left to say to you, Michael, are the ones I probably should have said to you a couple of years ago.' She held out her hand to him. 'Goodbye, Michael. I hope you make a name for yourself one day! With Wilky's help you probably will!'

But he refused to take her hand.

'What do you mean, goodbye?' he asked harshly.

'Just what the word usually means. It can be

very final, and in our case it couldn't be more so. I don't suppose I'll see you again after today, but I do wish you well. . . .' She felt suddenly that she was choking with sternly repressed emotion, and when she saw how shocked his eyes were she could have cried. 'It's been nice knowing you!'

He still refused to take her hand.

'You *are* leaving for Washington?' he demanded.

'On an early flight tomorrow morning.'

'You mean you're leaving . . . for good?'

'Definitely for good. My resignation from the nursing staff has already been accepted, and my services are being dispensed with immediately because I made a special request that I should be freed from duty at once. I wasn't exactly popular in a certain quarter for making such a request, but it was granted. I'm free as air now, with all obligation so far as the hospital is concerned behind me, and when I get to Washington I hope to start a new career.'

She told him all about the airline she hoped would be employing her before very long, and for the first time she felt a pang of real and acute regret when she saw how her words affected him. He actually turned very pale, and for a moment words seemed to fail him. And then he choked:

'You mean you're—going to fly all over the world?'

59

'As much of the world as they'll let me,' she responded light-heartedly (or so it must have struck him).

He turned several degrees paler.

'But you'll be based on Washington?'

'I expect so. But Washington's a good way from here!'

'It's a heck of a long way from here!'

There was silence between them for almost a full minute, and then he turned away from her and started pacing up and down. After another minute he returned to her.

'Sheelagh, we've got to talk this over, you and I——! Will you let me take you somewhere tonight where we can talk?'

'Where?'

'Oh, anywhere. . . .' He made rather a helpless gesture, which filled her with a kind of pity for him, for all at once he struck her as extremely vulnerable, and by no means as certain of himself and what he wanted from life as he wished her to believe—as he wanted himself to believe. 'What about Louis's?' naming one of their favourite ports of call.

She hesitated. She knew that it would be far wiser to refuse him outright, but some instinct that was stronger than herself—and which she blamed entirely on their past association—insisted that she at least give him a hearing. And after today, because her mind was made up, and she had no reason whatsoever to believe that his was any less made up than her own, they might never meet again. . . .

It was a sobering thought, and it shook her like a gust of wind. It left her feeling very sober indeed, very much as if the life blood itself was being drained from her.

'All right, Michael,' she said, and she said it as if the decision had been wrung from her.

Michael looked at her, long and hard.

'You agree that it shall be Louis's?' he asked.

In her turn she felt suddenly almost helpless. She looked back at him with a trace of appeal in her eyes.

'It's as good as anywhere else, isn't it?' she said. To her horror she realized that they had travelled miles in opposite directions since they were last at Louis's seafood restaurant. She repeated: 'It's as good as anywhere else!'

CHAPTER SIX

But at least in the past, when they spent the evening together, they had been able to show some obvious signs of pleasure in one another's company.

But tonight there was no pleasure, or none that would have been immediately obvious to an on-looker.

Sheelagh was still wearing the smart little suit she planned to wear for her departure from the hospital, and her hair looked very charming and shone beneath the lights of the restaurant. She seemed very composed, and although there was no longer anything antagonistic in her expression there was unmistakable resolve in her eyes, and her small chin was tip-tilted at such an angle that the resolve seemed to lend it a distinctly obstinate squareness.

Michael, studying her across the table, had the uneasy feeling that the battle was already lost. But he had to make some effort to get her to see reason.

'See here, honey——' he began, when their order had been given and Louis himself had bustled over to their table to make certain they were being properly taken care of. 'See here. . . . Listen to me!'

Sheelagh crumbled a roll on her plate. Her eyes returned his anxious gaze with a curiously gentle expression in her own.

'If you could would you marry me tomorrow, Michael?' she asked.

He flushed.

'If I could. . . .!'

'But you can't, can you? You take your orders from Wilky, and he says beware of little girls who want to shackle you with matrimonial ties, and remember you've a great future ahead of you!'

She reached a hand across the table and touched his, gently. 'Michael, I do honestly believe you're going to go way up and astonish the world by becoming a truly great surgeon, but I could have helped you to get there if you'd only trusted me a little and not felt so horribly afraid of all sorts of eventualities which might never become anything more than bogeys you've allowed to frighten you and ruin our little affair. For a wife *can* be a help to a husband, and I could have been a help to you . . .!'

'But if anything did go wrong and your career suffered as a result of marriage you would blame me for it, and because I know that I've come to terms with the unpleasant truth that you and I have no alternative ahead of us but to part. For you see, Michael, I'm not the waiting kind. . . . I'm demanding, and I want everything from you, and not a grudging half loaf. I want a *whole loaf—all* your trust and *all* your faith in me, and as I can't have either of those things I'm going away!'

His eyes reproached her bitterly.

'You could try waiting. I wouldn't be unreasonable. I know I couldn't expect you to wait for ever, but a year or two. . . .'

'You forget, Michael,' she reminded him, 'I would be a year or two older, and I might even change my mind about some things. You see, I'm only human, and if I knew you were not giving me everything you could I wouldn't guarantee it that I might not change my mind about you in the end! And that would be a sad thing after all we once thought we meant to one another . . . a horrible thing!

'I'd rather just go away and know that at least we parted without bitterness—and recriminations. For although I know I've said some horrible things to you since I found out about your promotion at least I didn't mean them. I love you, Michael. At the moment, with the knowledge that we're going to be separated very soon, I can't quite see how I'm ever going to fall *out* of love with you! Except that I know I've got to, and what better thing could I do, when I'm living with a problem of that sort, than go flying off round the world with so many other things to think about that I simply won't have the time to think about *you*!'

She leaned a little towards him, anxiously. 'Don't you see, Michael, it's the only thing I can *do*?'

He shook his head moodily, while attacking the food on his plate.

'You can, and you probably will, soon find somebody else to think about!'

'You mean fall in love with someone else?'

'Yes.'

She shook her head.

'I won't do that.' It was a kind of promise she made to him. 'Not yet, anyway. . . . Not for a long time. Probably never!'

He looked at her almost pityingly, his tired eyes adoring her. And the adoration was so open that she felt confused.

'My sweet Sheelagh, you know little or nothing about human nature. Go away from me— cut yourself deliberately off from my life—and there'll be nothing to prevent you falling in love with someone else. You're flesh and blood, not just a crisp uniform and a well-trained mind. . . .'

She flashed back at him angrily:

'I'm a woman who thought she had found her man, and had to step aside because her man preferred his chosen profession to a spot of home life and a future with her!'

Suddenly Michael's voice was insistent.

'Promise me one thing, Sheelagh! If your travels about the world fail to provide you with the distraction you're looking for. . . . If, for want of a better way of phrasing it, you find that you're unable to forget about me, and the man you could put in my place fails to measure up to everything you expect from him—for the simple reason that I was first, and although you might not want it to be so I've got a prior claim, you will let me know about it! You won't, in order to spite me, just marry someone else out of hand!'

'On the rebound, you mean?'

She smiled at him a little sadly, for even in the face of losing her he would not yield to temptation and say with the impulsiveness of a lover—not an ambitious doctor—the mere handful of words that would make it quite unnecessary for them to be parted at all.

A simple sentence, in fact, would cover it.

'Let's get married, Sheelagh! . . . Let's get married at once!'

If only, she thought, on a great gust of wistfulness, he would.

66

But he didn't, and she swallowed her disappointment with the utmost difficulty.

'Yes.'

Sheelagh sighed, and realized that she had crumbled the roll on her plate into something that resembled a little heap of sawdust.

'I give you my word,' she assured him solemnly, 'that I will not allow myself to be stampeded into marriage in order to get one back on you. But, on the other hand, should I meet a man with more to offer me than you have, then I might marry him . . . always providing I've fallen out of love with you!'

And the smile she directed at him across the table, covered with a bright check cloth and a little vase of flowers, was a mere travesty of the smile with which she usually rewarded him after supper at Louis's. It was a smile that made his heart ache, and about which he thought for a long time afterwards.

There seemed no point in spinning things out, so they said goodnight—which was virtually goodbye—to one another at an early hour, and Michael took her back to the nurses' home in a depressed mood which was perfectly understandable considering the circumstances, although the determination with which he clung to reason and those cold-blooded plans for his future so ap-

palled Sheelagh that she found it a comparatively
easy matter to say goodbye to him at her door.

She felt, as a matter of fact, that she was saying
goodbye to a stranger, and therefore there was
nothing peculiarly painful about the business.
She had spent an enlightening evening with him,
and any preconceived notions she had had about
the loyalties of a man who professed himself very
much in love had received a rude shock.

But apparently there were loyalties and loyalties.

CHAPTER SEVEN

SHEELAGH had no difficulty in recognizing Terry Fitzsimmons as she left the huge aircraft and walked across the tarmac of the capital's airport towards the exit gate. He was exactly like the photograph she had already seen of him, and his uniform identified him immediately. It was extremely smart, the pale blue of the sky that hung above the airport, and the twin rings on his sleeve signified his rank.

Sheelagh felt a momentary stirring of interest as she looked straight towards him. He was taller than she had expected, at least six feet in height, and it was possible that he was even more, with wide shoulders and a trim waist.

He was scanning the crowd anxiously, taking advantage of his height to see over the heads of the people in front of him. Sheelagh couldn't refrain from smiling a little. Fitzy had given him only the barest outline of what she looked like: 'A small blonde with a cute figure,' and she wondered how he could possibly recognize her from that.

But he did. She saw his eyes flick over her, hesitate, return to her and settle finally with an absurdly relieved expression on his face. He was not disappointed—she felt she could take it that he was thoroughly pleased with what he saw.

A wide grin split his attractive mouth open as he acknowledged her. He lifted his hand and waved, and she waved back, and then she was through the wire gate and he was holding her hand and welcoming her to Washington, D.C., telling her how glad he was to be able to help a friend of his sister.

'How about a little refreshment?' he suggested, taking her by the arm and guiding her out through the terminal, her case swinging from his free hand. 'I know how you feel when you climb down out of one of those things. The first place I make for is the nearest bar. Do you drink, by the way, or would you rather settle for a cup of java, or maybe a coke?'

He had a free-swinging way with him that went with his easy-going appearance. Quite unconsciously Sheelagh found herself likening him to Mike Kelman, for both men had the same happy disposition, so that she could almost have been with Michael as she allowed herself to be ushered into a cab and driven away from the airport. Sheelagh waited until they were settled, and were driving towards the city, before replying to his question.

As Fitzy had referred to him by his Christian

name she decided to call him by it from the outset.

'Terry, if you don't mind, I think I'd rather have coffee. About the only time I drink is at Christmas or at a party, and then I'm afraid I'm a two-drinks-all-night girl.'

'The kind of girl I like,' he grinned, taking Sheelagh's hand and squeezing it. 'Any girl who absorbs more than two in a night is a lush in my book. And it just so happens that I know the very spot. A cosy little place, where we can talk together, because apart from the fact that my sister thinks you're the sweetest and most lovable girl ever to don a cap and follow the honourable profession of nursing, I don't know a thing about you!'

He was as good as his word. The restaurant he took Sheelagh to was small and intimate, with subdued lighting and cool jazz filtering down from hidden speakers, filling the place with gentle background music.

Sheelagh suddenly discovered to her embarrassment that she was ravenously hungry. Without thinking she ordered a huge meal of steak and mushrooms, a crisp salad, Danish rolls, and for sweet, just to stop from dropping of malnutrition, apple pie and cream.

Terry listened as Sheelagh gave her order to the pert little coloured waitress with amused eyes.

He waited till the girl had jotted it all down, then ordered a cheese omelette and coffee for himself.

'You can't have any calorie problems,' he smiled when the waitress had gone. 'I'm beginning to see why you and Brenda are such good buddies. I bet you go on eating jags together!'

'I'm sorry,' Sheelagh felt herself blushing, 'I don't usually do things like that. I guess I just didn't realize how hungry I was.'

'Probably psychological—to get all profound. You've had it tough for a while, according to Brenda, now you're beginning to relax a little, and the tension that kept you from feeling like eating has suddenly disappeared, with the result you want to tuck in. Well, be my guest, there's nothing I like better than watching other people enjoy themselves.'

And Sheelagh did enjoy herself. The food was delicious, from the steak to the imaginative salad and the huge warm rolls, which she smothered liberally with butter and tangy blue-vein cheese. As for the apple pie, she had tasted nothing like it since leaving home, for when her mother had been alive she excelled at pastries of all kinds. Sheelagh and her sister had grown up with a deep fondness for such delicacies. She decided she would have to come to the little restaurant again. Over coffee, they got to talking about the job

Terry had in mind for her. It was as nurse-hostess.

This was something comparatively new for the line Terry flew for. All the major airlines had access to trained nurses should the request be made, and many hostesses had had nurses' training, though, according to Terry, very few had gone right through and become registered, ducking out after the first year or maybe two.

'You see,' he said after he had finished outlining his ideas for her, 'we often carry elderly people who require, or really should have, the services of a fully trained nurse. I remember one trip we made, through to the Far East—Bangkok, Manila, that part of the world. An old fellow became ill and we had to put down, get him off to a hospital. The closest field was somewhere in Vietnam, and we very nearly piled up using it. It was built for piston-engined kites, not jets.'

'And the passenger, the old man?'

'He died.' Terry made a face and took a quick drink of his coffee. 'I don't know if having someone like you aboard would have perhaps saved him, or whether he would have died anyway. But at least we wouldn't have felt forced to put down at a place like that, almost in the middle of the fighting, jeopardizing the lives of everyone aboard.

'Sometimes, of course, there's a doctor

amongst the passengers, and that helps. But I doubt if any airline will ever get around to making it a rule to carry a doctor as a permanent member of the crew,' he added, putting down his cup and grinning crookedly. 'They're all for cutting down on expenditure as it is. If they had their way, there would only be one pilot, and he could double for navigator, and maybe even engineer, into the bargain.'

They talked about the personal qualifications that were required to land a job as hostess. They were pretty awe-inspiring, and Sheelagh began to have second doubts. High school graduation was required, plus two years of college. Although Sheelagh never got to college, she hoped that her nurses' training would get her through, by-passing the college bit. Applicants had to be attractive and poised, Terry Fitzsimmons said, and above all they had to be resourceful and tactful.

Here again Sheelagh could only hope that her hospital training would get her through, for one certainly had to be resourceful when in charge of a ward, and tact was something that went hand-in-glove with being a nurse. It was only too easy to quarrel with some of the cantankerous old so-and-sos of patients one so often collected, especially in the women's ward.

There was very keen competition for the jobs,

apparently, which was something Sheelagh had always suspected. Most girls regarded it as being very much of a glamour job, although according to Terry there was a very high turnover rate. Many of the hostesses landed rich husbands from among the big business executives who habitually jetted around the world.

Ages required were between twenty and twenty-seven; height was between five feet two inches to five feet eight inches, with weight in proportion to height. Applicants had to be in excellent health, and had to prove a background virtually free from sickness.

'And how long will I be in training?' Sheelagh asked when Terry paused for breath, signalling across their waitress for two more coffees. She had had her fill of going to classes and lectures, and the thought of once again attending school, being treated like a student, was not a particularly appealing one.

'About five weeks,' he replied, grinning as though he had read her mind, 'and you don't look particularly crazy about the idea, either.'

'I guess because I think I've had my share of classrooms,' Sheelagh smiled back, liking him, thinking again how much he resembled Mike Kelman. Thinking of Michael was a mistake. The sharp ache that she had first experienced when

she had been walking in the night, alone, along
Fisherman's Wharf, returned, driving deep into
her heart and seeming to twist there, adding to
her sudden agony.

Sheelagh gave a little choked cry and lurched
forward against the table, her hands clutching at
her chest as though to pluck out the pain. Terry
was on his feet in an instant, reaching out, gripping her shoulders.

'Sheelagh, what is it? What's the matter? Are
you ill? . . . Sheelagh, I'd better go find a doctor!'

'No!' Sheelagh somehow managed to look up at
him, even managed to smile. 'Don't be silly, I'm all
right—just indigestion, the price you pay for making a pig of yourself. That was quite a meal I ate!'

'Well,' he sat down again—reluctantly, his face
mirroring his concern, putting frown lines across
the wide, intelligent forehead, darkening the blue
eyes so that they were suddenly identical to
Fitzy's, 'okay, if you're sure you're all right.'

'Stop worrying, for heaven's sake.' Sheelagh
forced herself to sit upright, folding her hands in
her lap, keeping the smile fixed on her lips,
frozen there while she waited for the pain to diminish. And slowly it did, her therapy of self-will
paid off, and Michael's image slowly faded from
her mind. 'Now,' she said briskly, 'we were talking about the training, weren't we?'

He relaxed then, nodding, smiling back at Sheelagh. 'We were. You were telling me you were more than a little sick of sitting in class-rooms. Well, I shouldn't worry too much, it's not that sort of training at all, in fact I think you'll find it all rather fun.'

'Providing, of course,' Sheelagh reminded him, 'they accept me.'

'I spoke to our personnel manager before ever I met you, young lady, and he's tickled pink to be getting an R.N. on his list, so if I were you I'd stop worrying about whether or not you're going to be accepted.'

'I can't believe it's all that simple,' Sheelagh laughed, 'or that any personnel manager of a major airline would so fall over himself to get a common-or-garden nurse to come and work for him. I suspect, Terry, that you pull not a little weight at that head office of yours.'

He chuckled, shaking his head, grinning widely, his blue eyes twinkling so that he looked quite the most handsome male in the whole rest-aurant, and most probably, Sheelagh thought, in the whole of Washington.

The waitress came back with their two coffees, and he thanked her, waited for her to go away, and picked up the conversation where they had left off. 'You'll make me swollen-headed, Sheelagh, make me begin to think I'm something more than a young and very junior co-pilot, that I'm maybe a captain with fifteen years' solid experience in back of me and God knows how many thousands of hours of flying time to my credit. Is this your line? Is this the way you kid all your boy-friends along? And I'll bet there must be an army of them, too. I guarantee just about every doctor at that hospital of yours is crazy about you. How many broken hearts did you leave behind, Sheelagh, or couldn't you count them?'

Sheelagh just stared at him, silent and angry. He hadn't meant anything; it had been harmless and completely innocent kidding. But he had once again allowed the pain to return, this time a slower, deeper sort of pain, that attacked not only her heart but her entire body and most of her mind, seizing and then gripping her remorselessly.

'There was only one,' she heard herself say in a slow-motion sort of voice that frightened her, for it did not sound like her own voice at all. 'There was never an army, Terry.'

'I'm sorry,' he sobered instantly, his voice, his eyes, his expression immediately contrite. 'I guess I touched the raw spot, didn't I? Is he the reason for you leaving the hospital?'

Sheelagh nodded, not trusting herself to speak.

'I see!' he looked down at his cup, stirring the coffee around and around, although he had not as yet put any sugar in it. 'Like that, huh, running away from memories?'

'I guess we all do at one time or another, Terry.'

'I won't ask about him, at least not right now,' he looked up at her quickly, and his gaze seemed to see clear through into Sheelagh's mind, 'because it obviously isn't something you want to talk about. But later, when you're settled in and I think you might be a little more in the mood, then I want to hear about this guy of yours. Because, quite frankly, I have every intention of moving in and taking over where he left off!'

CHAPTER EIGHT

TERRY'S words were to occur again and again to Sheelagh during the weeks of training that were to make her, not only a good flying nurse, but also a first-class hostess.

Terry never mentioned either her unhappy affair or his intentions towards her again that day.

He had already found her a small apartment in Georgetown, D.C, a residential suburb of the capital, and one of the most historic sections of the city. It was a charming little one-room affair close to the famous Georgetown University. From her window Sheelagh could see the clock-tower of the University with its handsome spired roof. She did not have to worry about buying an alarm clock herself, for it chimed the hours and half-hours and always woke her up in time to shower and dress, make a quick snack, and get along to the classes.

He took her to the apartment as soon as they'd finished their coffee, introducing her to the landlady, a Mrs Newman, a stout, homely woman with an ever-present smile who seemed thrilled to be having a nurse-soon-to-become-an-air-hostess living in her house.

Everything went exactly as Terry had predicted it would. The personnel manager was charm itself. The rigid medical Sheelagh had to undergo showed her health to be perfect, so, with her nursing credentials and the letters of recommendation she had from the hospitals she'd worked in, there was nothing to hold her up. Before she knew it she was being fitted for the smart blue hostess's uniform she would be wearing from then on, and she was instructed to report at the airline's main office building the following morning to begin her training.

And, again as Terry had predicted, the training period *was* fun. The airline had training down to a fine art. Everything went like clockwork, something they had found very necessary, Sheelagh presumed, in view of their large turnover of girls. It must have been heartbreaking for the instructors to see the girls they had worked so hard with leave the airline after sometimes only a couple of weeks, once they had captured a rich and handsome husband for themselves.

There were mock-ups of the interiors of the three types of aircraft the airline owned; the huge turbo-jets, the Boeings, the Convairs, the Comets, Douglas, Caravelle and Supersonic planes. Then came the turbo-props—the Avros, Canadair and Electras. Finally the piston-engined kites (everyone referred to the aircraft as kites, from the flying crews down to the most junior mechanic, and Sheelagh soon got into the habit); these were the slower planes, used, mainly within the U.S. and Canada. They were the Convairs and Lockheeds, though Terry told her they were frequently used as transports, when they flew the trans-ocean runs and the polar routes.

The interior of these mock-ups were complete to the smallest detail, from the seats and doors, down to the galley and pantry, with their bottles and tiny ovens and grills, even the inevitable paper bags.

The course was a very thorough one, starting off with first-aid, something Sheelagh could well have been excused from because she had learned all of it during her first few weeks of nursing. It took in such things as the comfort of passengers, sleeper seats and sleeperettes, emergency drill, landing, take-off. It also included the briefing of passengers on position and landing times, safety-belt and smoking, schedules, rosters, everything, in fact, they were ever likely to be called upon to know.

Out of all the girls going through with her, Sheelagh found herself drawn towards a very good-looking redhead with green eyes and a perfect figure, named Aileen Roder. She came from Philadelphia, where her people lived. But as soon s she was out of college she'd decided that she wanted to fly and so had applied for a position with the airline. And the way she told it, Sheelagh suspected that she hadn't been able to get away from parental control soon enough.

'Well, what will we do in the way of a celebration when we're honest-to-goodness hostesses?' she asked one afternoon towards the end of the course when she and Sheelagh were relaxing in the canteen with a coke. 'I'd like to tie on a bit of a wing-ding, wouldn't you?'

'Think we've deserved it?' Sheelagh smiled, comparing the few weeks of what to her had been fun with the rigorous demands of a nursing course.

'Deserved or not, it's the thing to do when you finish a course, any course. How about it? I'd rather like for us to do it alone, with maybe a couple of well-heeled males to supply the wherewithal, rather than get mixed up in a big crowd of girls.'

'Who did you have in mind?' Sheelagh asked, taking a long pull through her straw and glancing around the busy canteen at the pilots and their crews as they came and went. Each group moved separately, entering and leaving together, so that they reminded Sheelagh of a lot of little armies getting shuffled around.

'You mean for escorts:' Aileen lifted one beautiful brow and looked at Sheelagh with her emerald-green eyes. She was very beautiful, Sheelagh thought as she nodded in reply, wondering just how long it would be before her new friend found herself a wealthy young executive or stockbroker eager to support her for the rest of her life. 'I don't know,' Aileen tossed her head in mild irritation, her long hair moving out like a spreading fan with the movement. 'That's no problem, is it? We're neither of us exactly ugly, honey.'

'You sound very confident,' Sheelagh smiled, finishing her coke and pushing the bottle away from her. 'Is it really as easy as that? Don't you think we ought to be a little careful?'

'Well, darling, we're not going to make eyes at some fat old man with teenage kids, now are we? Washington's filled with handsome and very eligible young men, from diplomats to marine officers.'

Sheelagh thought of Terry then, of what he had said on that first day in Washington. How would he feel, she wondered, after making his intentions so plain, to hear she had gone out on a date with someone else, a stranger that Aileen Roder had picked up, a meal-ticket, virtually somebody to pay for their passing-out celebration?

'I think I know who I'd like to bring along,' she said softly, feeling more than a littled awed by her friend's worldliness. 'He's one of our pilots.'

'That gorgeous-looking thing with the blond hair and simply divine blue eyes?' Aileen wanted to know, her huge green eyes sweeping over Sheelagh's face searchingly, as though seeing her for the first time. 'The one who's for ever popping in and grinning at you when you're supposed to be learning how to take care of a fat man with a slipped disc who can't get himself up out of his seat, or something equally ghastly?'

'That's the one,' Sheelagh agreed, chuckling at Aileen's send-up of the subject for one of their recent lessons—the taking care of physically-handicapped passengers. 'If you like I'll see if he has a friend.'

'Thanks all the same, and you're an absolute pet,' Aileen gave a huge, theatrical sort of smile, 'but I make it a rule, darling, to always pick up my own men. That way I know exactly what I'm getting. Although I must confess to having had one or two nasty surprises, which just goes to show, I guess, that you can't always pick a book by its cover.'

Sheelagh found herself laughing, something she did frequently when she was with Aileen Roder. Although she was only twenty-one, Aileen behaved like a woman of forty, like somebody with more than twenty years of experience with the opposite sex behind her. Sheelagh loved the way she talked, like a Broadway actress, a second Bankhead, in fact. Which was by way of being amazing when one considered that the closest Aileen had come to Broadway and the professional theatre was a little dramatic acting when she was at college. But she was fun.

She was what Sheelagh needed, for her ache for Michael was still a very real thing, especially when she was alone in her tiny apartment, alone with her thoughts and memories.

'Okay then,' Aileen said, slipping to her feet. 'You get your guy set up and I'll take care of mine. And we'll make it the night we finish training, which—unless something happens to throw the syllabus for a loop—is next Friday. Just three days away.'

And so it was agreed, the big night was Friday night. The day on which Sheelagh officially became a nurse-hostess.

Friday did not take long to arrive, and Terry, when he called at Sheelagh's flat, looked very handsome and wonderfully masculine in a light grey sharkskin suit, white shirt, narrow black tie. Looked, in fact, exactly as the artists working for the advertising agencies usually portrayed jet pilots on the airline posters. Big, brave and smiling a wide grin of challenge at the world.

Because she felt passing out as a hostess successfully was something of an occasion and because she felt she owed it to Terry for his kindness, for without him she would still be back in 'Frisco working as a nurse, Sheelagh had splurged on a bottle of champagne for them to celebrate with alone before meeting up with the others, Aileen and her 'mystery date'. Apart from dropping the fact that her man-of-the-evening was not an American, but hinting that he was something special, Aileen had kept Sheelagh guessing who the last member of the foursome was to be.

'Well!' Terry exclaimed, when, after receiving his sisterly kiss of greeting, Sheelagh went to the tiny fridge her apartment boasted and produced her bottle all ready to be opened, and with a starchy white napkin already wrapped around it. 'Whose wedding anniversary are we celebrating? Champagne! They must pay you girls a lot better than they pay us, for Pete's sake!'

'Three hundred dollas a month for eighty-five hours' flying time and thirty-five hours' ground duties, and you know it,' Sheelagh laughed as she passed the champagne to him to open. 'Only we're not flying yet, so we only get two-fifty. Now open that up . . . I'm thirsty!'

'Thought you weren't a drinking kind of gal?' he chuckled as he twisted free the wire and began working at the cork.

'Champagne isn't drinking, it's a way of life,' Sheelagh quipped, feeling happier than she could remember for what seemed a very long time. Somehow Michael's ghost, which had haunted her happiness for so long, seemed to have entirely gone, had disappeared completely, leaving Sheelagh feeling very bright and girlish . . . and wonderfully free. 'So just you hurry up and get that cork out, my man,' she laughed, 'because tonight I want to live a little.'

'If madame would be so good as to bear with me a moment longer,' Terry chuckled, going along with Sheelagh's mood as he struggled with the obstinate cork, 'for, in truth, I had no idea what racy company I was keeping!'

The cork came out with a plop and Terry managed to get the fizzy wine into the two tumblers which were all Sheelagh had, without spilling too much on the carpet.

'Well, cheers, bung-ho, down the hatch,' Terry grinned, speaking with a pseudo-English accent, clinking his glass against Sheelagh's, then lifting it high in a toast. 'What are we drinking to, exactly? The fact that the prettiest little nurse in Washington has agreed to join the airline?'

'That'll do for a start,' Sheelagh laughed, 'and stop going all English on me, showing off because you've travelled around and seen the world.'

'Unintentional, m'dear,' he said, still using his mock British accent, 'frightfully sorry and all that sort of rot. Right-oh, then, we'll just say *Skoal* and enjoy the bally stuff, what?'

'*Skoal!*' Sheelagh repeated, trying not to sneeze as she lifted the fizzing wine to her lips.

Aileen's date turned out to be something really terrific. His name was Louis Salvatore Castellano, and he was with the Italian Embassy, working out from Massachusetts Avenue, commonly known as Embassy Row.

Louis Castellano was every girl's romantic notion of what a well-bred Italian male should be, Sheelagh thought as she looked him over while Aileen made the introductions. The face was one of almost classical male beauty, from the straight, sensitive nose to the high, intelligent forehead and firm chin below the wide, humorous mouth, with the black and wavy hair setting off the picture and adding the touch of perfection.

And the body, Sheelagh could not help but

noting, went perfectly with the head. Tall and lithe, Louis Castellano moved with panther-like grace, his every motion, every gesture smooth and fluid-like. He was, in a word, sensational.

They had agreed to meet outside the Freer Gallery of Art, for apparently the Italian Government was loaning the gallery some paintings and pieces of ancient sculpture and Louis had been making the final arrangements concerning their transportation and insurance.

It was early evening—just after seven, and the sun had not completely gone. The capital's famous monuments and landmarks stood bathed in gentle light, something that Sheelagh got quite a kick from during the cab ride down from her apartment, for she had been so busy with the course she had hardly had time to make the usual tourist's sight-seeing tours.

'My, but don't we look lovely!' Aileen exclaimed, giving Sheelagh a long look of appraisal, finally, when everyone knew who everyone else was.

'Thanks,' Sheelagh smiled nervously, feeling her cheeks begin to burn, for Aileen's comment had caused both Terry and the young Italian diplomat to turn and openly ogle her. 'It's old . . . I've had it for years.'

It was not exactly the truth, for Sheelagh had

decided upon the red chiffon dress for the evening, a dress that she had bought less than three months back for a date with Michael. It had been his birthday, and she had wanted to look her best. And it did, she knew, do something for her, emphasizing her blondeness and strawberries-and-cream complexion—something, she supposed, she had to thank her Irish ancestors for. Sheelagh looked, then, at Aileen. As usual, she was beautifully gowned, a nile-green number that contrasted beautifully with her long red hair, while at the same time managing to highlight her green eyes.

'We're lucky men, Louis,' Terry winked at the handsome Italian, 'I'll bet we're the envy of Washington with these two.'

'You are both very very beautiful,' Louis said formally, bowing slightly and smiling at Aileen and Sheelagh—an old-world gesture that somehow seemed to be perfect. 'As you say, Terry, we are privileged and honoured to enjoy their company.'

It was quite a speech, but in the way in which Louis said it made it all sound perfectly natural. He spoke with scarcely an accent, so that, had she been asked, Sheelagh would have said he was English rather than Italian.

She glanced at Terry from the corner of her

eye. He was looking at the Italian with a frowning expression on his face, and it occurred to her that perhaps something as smooth as Louis Castellano would not be terribly popular with members of his own sex. He was strictly a box-office edition, she decided, just the type of man, in fact, who would appeal to somebody like Aileen.

'Well, darlings,' Aileen, as usual, proceeded to take charge of things, 'let's go eat, shall we? Where do you two handsome male creatures plan to take us?' She looked first at Louis, standing beside her, gripping her tightly by the hand, then at Terry. 'Any lovely surprises? Because this is, as you know, a night for celebration . . . Sheelagh and I are now fully-fledged hostesses with the world at our feet. Right, Terry?' she smiled a wide and winning smile at the pilot, her lovely green eyes opening to their fullest extent—a disarming gaze that was at once both an invitation and a challenge.

'Right,' Terry affirmed, not looking terribly happy about things and making no attempt to suggest an eatery.

'Why don't we go to that lovely place you took me to when I first arrived in town?' Sheelagh said quickly, feeling that she had to come to Terry's aid. 'Where I made such a pig of myself with their divine food?'

'I don't somehow think,' Terry said slowly, looking Aileen over closely, a head-to-toe-and-back-again scrutiny that came close to being rude and embarrassing, 'that Aileen would enjoy that spot terribly much. I kind of think we should get a little more ambitious.'

Aileen caught the sarcasm and Sheelagh saw her face set into a tight mask, the green eyes narrowing as she stared back at Terry. Then, as quickly as it had come, it faded, and once again she was the wide-smiling personality girl.

'Very well, darling, if you think we're worth something a little better this evening, who am I to insist? We're in your hands.' She pulled Louis to her, hugging his arm to show that he was included in her suggestion. 'Whatever you decide upon I'm certain will be absolutely wonderful and madly exciting.'

'May I, perhaps, suggest somewhere?' Louis asked when Terry did not seem as though he was going to name anywhere 'absolutely wonderful and madly exciting'.

'But of course, darling!' Aileen exclaimed, cuddling up to her date and pressing her face against his shoulder. 'I'm sure you diplomatic types know some really marvellous spots.'

'If you like Italian food I think perhaps you'll enjoy it,' Louis said, talking directly at Sheelagh and Terry. 'It's called the Via del Corso, which happens to be the name of a street in Rome in which the uncle of the proprietor owns a restaurant. They serve excellent meals, and their wine is specially brought in from California, from vineyards owned by yet another uncle of the proprietor.'

'Sounds wonderful, darling!' Aileen said, smiling brightly.

'Any music?' Terry asked.

'Italian-style only, I'm afraid, but it has a very good atmosphere, and if you feel like singing and know Italian songs you go right ahead and sing . . . everybody else does.'

'You've sold us,' Sheelagh smiled, 'so lead the way, Louis!'

The Via del Corso looked as though it had been transported from Rome and set up in Washington, D.C. It was about as Italian-looking as any restaurant could look, with red-and-white checked table-clothes, candlesticks made of empty wine bottles, and travel posters showing off the scenic beauties of Italy. There were even bunches of dried herbs and garlic hanging from the low-raftered ceiling.

Although it was packed, the proprietor, an enormously fat man with a bald head and a drooping black moustache that reminded Sheelagh of Marlon Brando made up to look like a Mexican bandit, welcomed them with open arms. He found them a table from which they could see all around the huge room and across the dancing area that was situated before the raised dais that housed the musicians—three violins and two accordions, all five men working hard over their instruments, producing a fast, driving, very Italian-sounding music.

The food was all that Louis had claimed. They drank smooth Cinzano aperitif, and they allowed Louis to order for them. Sheelagh had something called *Spaghetti alla carbonara*, while Aileen and Terry settled for roast lamb basted with wine imported from the Castelli. Louis, who claimed he had had a large meal midday, ate a colourful *insalata*—an Italian-style salad, something that looked so good that Sheelagh shared one with Aileen to finish off their meal, enjoying one that Louis called a *capricciosos*. Then they sipped *caffe ristretto*, the very strong and black coffee that only Italians seem to know how to make.

The evening passed as though on wings. Almost before Sheelagh knew it, it was twelve o'clock. The main lights were turned off, the only illumination being the candles that graced every table. And it was exactly as Louis had claimed—

everyone sang, and if they didn't know the words they *la-la-la'ed* their way through the song. Sheelagh was not in the least surprised to discover Louis Castellano was a superb dancer. He led her through the strange steps of the Italian dances with an effortless grace that inspired confidence so that Sheelagh felt as though she had been dancing to Italian music all her life.

'Aileen tells me that you are a nurse,' he said as they did a slow number as a change from the more hectic dancing, keeping to the fringes of the floor so as not to hamper the more enthusiastic dancers sticking to local convention. Sheelagh admitted to the charge, practically out of breath after the strenuous activities the driving colourful music demanded.

'I have always admired nurses and nursing, in fact all facets of the medical profession, very much,' Louis went on, his dark eyes seeming to bore into Sheelagh's in a very primitive but at the same time well-disguised challenge. 'In fact, if it were possible to have one's time over again, I think I'd be a doctor instead of a diplomat. It must be very satisfying work.'

'It's not the glamour job the movies and TV shows imply it is, I assure you,' Sheelagh smiled, feeling a sudden fluttery uncertainty before his so very masculine personality, the arrogance that was in itself magnetic. 'Ninety-nine per cent of the time it's just plain hard work.'

'Nevertheless,' Louis insisted, his arms and shoulders working rhythmically as he did an expert, almost professionally perfect step, 'I still maintain that it offers a man, or woman, more than my chosen career.'

Sheelagh shrugged and looked away. Speaking about it had brought memories of hospital life back to her, had caused her mind to flash back to her room in nurses' quarters, to Fitzy, and, of course, to Michael. Had she done the right thing in packing up and leaving? she wondered, beginning to know all the bitter, painful pangs of uncertainty that so frequently follow a hasty decision. Now she was a hostess, she would be travelling, seeing the world, and—who knew?—perhaps finding herself a wealthy, wonderful husband like so many air hostesses were supposed to do.

Was that what she wanted? Sheelagh wondered, being honest with herself for the first time. Nursing was what she had been trained to do, was what she had always wanted to do. Had it been a mistake, coming to Washington, flying out on her problem, *their* problem, Michael's and her own?

From that moment on the night was spoiled.

Michael was back in her thoughts, his image superimposed over the faces of both Terry and Louis, who, whenever he got the chance, indulged in a mild flirtation, taking care that Aileen and Terry were out of earshot before doing so. But Sheelagh barely noticed his overtures. He was not her type, handsome though he may have been, smooth-mannered as he undoubtedly was. She was not drawn to such men, for despite his powerful physique and strong features, Louis Castellano looked too much like a male model to appeal to Sheelagh, who liked her men to do something useful with their lives.

Her mood was quickly recognized by the others, especially Aileen, who seemed to have a perceptiveness in such things. She leaned across the table when they were all sitting down at the end of a dance, touching Sheelagh's arm with her fingers.

'Honey, you getting tired? You look beat!'

'I am a little weary,' Sheelagh confessed, smiling briefly, mildly surprised at Aileen's apparently sincere concern. 'I guess if you two don't mind I might try and talk Terry into taking me home . . . okay, Terry?' she looked at the pilot as she spoke, noticing that he had been watching her with a troubled, thoughtful expression.

'Naturally! Any time!' he glanced at Aileen, then

Louis. 'So if you two will excuse us, I'll take one weary nurse home. I guess the thought of becoming a fully-fledged hostess is just a little too much for her!'

They said their goodbyes and left, although Sheelagh somehow got the impression that Louis was not terribly happy about it, that he would have preferred for them to have sat it out.

It was well after two before they finally reached Sheelagh's apartment. Terry stood on the threshold, waiting to be asked in. Sheelagh, looking up into the tanned, handsome face, found herself wondering about the pilot, for despite his warning that he intended moving in, taking over where Michael had left off, he had so far made no attempt to do so, had never gone beyond a polite and utterly sexless peck on the cheek. Now, looking up into his blue eyes, Sheelagh recognized the hungry, intense look of an amorously-inclined male. Recognized that that particular phase of their relationship was over, that now, from this moment on, it was strictly a man-woman affair. Not a 'friend-of-my-sister' thing.

'Coffee?' he nodded hintingly over Sheelagh's shoulder towards the tiny hot-plate that, together with the minute fridge, went with the apartment.

'It's very late, Terry,' Sheelagh heard herself say, uttering the time-honoured excuse for an overly-persuasive escort.

'Not *that* late . . . you can spare me the time it takes to make one lil' ol' cup, surely! If you use instant coffee, one instant!'

Sheelagh smiled, nodding. It was difficult to refuse in the face of such a logical argument. 'Okay, one cup!'

He sat in the tiny armchair and watched her while she switched on the jug, set out the cups and saucers, found crackers and spread them out on a small plate.

'How'd it go, anyway?' he asked, stretching out his long legs and unbuttoning his jacket, 'the evening, I mean.'

'Fine!' Sheelagh turned and smiled at him. 'I had a ball . . . thank you very much, Terry, it was a lot of fun.'

'Thank *you* very much, you were far and away the most luscious dish there, your friend Aileen notwithstanding.'

'You don't like her very much, do you?' Sheelagh asked, remembering the mild clashing of temperaments that had occurred earlier on.

'She's inclined to be a bit of a phoney,' Terry admitted, nodding slightly. 'Sorry, I know you've buddied up with her, but you did ask me a straight-out question.'

'And I got a straight-out answer,' Sheelagh agreed. 'How about Louis?'

'How about Louis?'

'What did you think of him?'

'What is this, some kind of personality quiz?' Terry grinned his big grin, watching Sheelagh as she dropped on to the bed and kicked off her shoes, felt around beneath it with her stockinged feet for her mules. 'Let's just say he's not really a man's man, huh? He was okay, I guess.'

'So all in all you didn't really have such a good time,' Sheelagh, feeling much more comfortable out of her spike heels, commented. 'I'm sorry.'

'Who said I didn't have a good time, kid? You were there, weren't you? That made the evening as far as I'm concerned.'

Sheelagh felt herself begin to colour and looked away, away from the boldness of his wide-spaced blue eyes. She would have to be careful, it was two a.m. and they were alone together in her apartment. Under such circumstances, it didn't take a guy very long to start getting ideas.

The electric jug began to splutter and Sheelagh, grateful for the excuse to break things up, sprang to her feet and hastily made the coffee. 'Sugar? Cream?' she turned, looking at him over her shoulder, as she asked the question. He was looking at her admiringly, his gaze roving appreciatively over her figure.

'Huh?' he asked vaguely, lifting his brows and

somehow forcing his eyes to drift up to Shee-lagh's face.

'White or black? With or without?' she said a trifle sharply, knowing that her cheeks were burning.

'Black, and without, I've got a lot of alcohol to drench out of my system. That wine's all right in small doses, but when you're on it all night . . .!' he clapped his hand to his forehead and rolled his eyes in mock agony.

'You're as sober as a judge and you know it,' Sheelagh laughed as she set the cup and saucer, the plate containing the crackers down beside him on the floor.

'Yeah, that's right,' he reached out quickly, his fingers gripping around Sheelagh's wrist as she began to stand erect again, his face inches from her own. 'I'm sober as a judge, Sheelagh, and I want you to remember that, okay?'

'Please!' Sheelagh exclaimed, beginning to feel more than a little apprehensive. 'Terry, you're hurting me!'

'Sorry!' he released her as suddenly as he had seized her, watching as Sheelagh moved back to the bed, to where her own cup of coffee stood. 'I'm *very* sorry, as a matter of fact,' he added, his voice gentle and sincere, the eyes worried, as though at any moment he expected to be thrown out of the apartment. 'But I've something to say, something hellishly important, at least to me, and I wouldn't care to think that perhaps I get to sound like a drunk when I finally speak up.'

Sheelagh remained silent. There was nothing to say. She had been right, then, Terry had been a good boy long enough. Now their friendship was about to enter into the second, more positive stage, was about to become a true man-woman relationship. And there was nothing—absolutely nothing in the sweet, wide world that she could do about it.

Even had she wanted to.

CHAPTER NINE

THE feel, the taste of Terry's kiss, remained with Sheelagh long after he had gone—a haunting, lingering mixture of sensations that was, to say the least, disturbing. It had happened naturally, swiftly, inevitably. The 'something hellishly important' that he had had to say had been approximately what Sheelagh had anticipated, had halfway to expected.

From the very first moment, Terry had claimed, when he had first seen her at the airport, he had felt himself tremendously drawn to Sheelagh as a person. But purposely he had taken his time, had not rushed things, and tried to allow her time to get over whatever—or *who*ever—it was she had come to Washington to escape from. But now, he had whispered as he swept her tight into his arms, his lips hovering scant inches above Sheelagh's mouth, he felt he had waited quite long enough. He had to do what he had wanted to do from that first meeting. And he had. And Sheelagh enjoyed it immensely, closing her eyes and surrendering to the delicious thrill of the moment.

She had not struggled, had not protested in any

way, and he had done her the honour of not following up on her preliminary submission, but of being content with that one kiss.

He had gone then, promising to ring, his grin wide his personality lifted to almost boyish heights, so that he had positively bounced out of her apartment.

So now she had another problem, Sheelagh mused as she lay in bed, watching the lightening skies tint the windows and the mirror of the dressing table, pushing tentatively at shadows and dreams. Lazily, then, she stretched her arm up into a trembling band of sunlight streaming across her bed, relishing the unfettered moment on the border of sleep and wakefulness when the problems of living still lie relatively, mercifully dormant. This new thing, this fresh angle that had entered her life, seemed not so much—as it was—the corner of a triangle, but an intriguing, dreamlike complication, very much an *affaire de cœur*, as the French put it—an affair of the heart, with a typical Gallic lightness about it.

And then, as the sunlight strengthened, so did her awareness of what she had done, what Terry's kiss had really meant. Sheelagh sat up with a start, staring at the wall opposite her bed, taking in every detail of the patterned wallpaper, as though, in its complicated floral design, she could somehow read the answer to this, her new problem.

She felt guilty and frightened together. She loved Michael, she knew that, accepted the fact without reservation . . . and yet here she was becoming involved with another man! All right, Sheelagh thought, hugging her arms tight around herself, trying to be logical and determined together, to think the thing through. So then how did she feel about Terry Fitzsimmons?

She was attracted to him, what woman wouldn't be? For he was young, tall and handsome, besides being an awful lot of fun. And did she *really* want to become involved with him?

And then, of course, there was Fitzy to consider. Sheelagh felt a deep affection for her plump, tragically plain room-mate, and, in addition, she owed her a lot for providing the means of escape from what had become an intolerable situation. And so, under such circumstances, considering each and every factor involved, how could she possibly hurt Fitzy's brother who, in his turn, had been equally kind to her, if not more so?

Sheelagh groaned and kicked the covers from her, jumping out of bed and making for the tiny shower stall. She had fled from one seemingly impossible problem only to become enmeshed in another.

All right then, Sheelagh decided as the warm

water spurted down over her, she would have to do what she had done before, when other problems had presented themselves. She would immerse herself completely in her work. She would become the best darn jet nurse in the business!

Because she was an R.N., Sheelagh found herself detailed immediately to the jets flying the international lines, by-passing the local-service airlines, something that, she learned later, was decidedly unusual for a newcomer.

A cruel fate designed that Sheelagh's first trip would be a transpolar one, the short cut over the North Pole that cut hundreds of miles off the more orthodox routes, her take-off point being San Francisco; her final destinatton, Paris.

Sheelagh could only sit and stare in utter disbelief at the traffic control officer who had briefed the crew of the jet that she had been detailed to, unable to believe her own ears as he set out the flight plan they would be following.

'Frisco! Michael, and all the things she had been at pains to escape from! It wasn't, couldn't be true, they were playing some sort of joke on her, surely . . . they just *had* to be! But one look at the businesslike, no-nonsense face of the traffic control officer told her that she could stop fooling herself. It was true, all right, terribly, shockingly true. She was going back to San Francisco, like it or not.

Sheelagh waited until the other members of the crew had filed from the small room at the completion of the briefing, and then rose and approached the traffic officer, ensconced behind an item of furniture that was midway between a desk and a lectern.

He was a short, sandy-haired man in his early forties. He nodded and smiled as she came and stood in front of him. 'Well, all set for your first trip, Nurse?' he asked, the smile stretching into a friendly grin. 'Nervous, I suppose.'

'A little,' Sheelagh admitted. 'I was really wondering why it is that I've been detailed to make the long flights so soon, sir. I believe it's rather unusual.'

'It is,' he agreed, nodding shortly. 'But you happen to be a fully qualified nurse with excellent references, and, believe it or not, we don't seem to get many nurses willing to forsake their precious hospitals for the sort of roving, romantic life we offer a girl. Frankly, I can't think why— dedication, I suppose, the professional kind that writers are always writing about but that I never really believed in until I saw it with my own eyes. Why, I've seen airlines make absolutely marvellous offers to nurses, only to be turned down cold.'

'I take it, then,' Sheelagh said a little hurriedly, beginning to feel guilty about having left her job and the hospital in the face of his speech about dedicated nurses who, it seemed, were only a hop-skip and a jump behind Florence Nightingale herself, 'you have a few fairly sick passengers scheduled to make the flight.'

'That's right.' He nodded and smiled again, his clear grey eyes beginning to glance over Sheelagh's figure appreciatively. 'Two, in actual fact. Nothing terribly serious, but one of them, the woman, insisted that she have the services of someone like yourself. That's why we decided to break a few rules, skip over the usual routine, and let your first flight be a big one.'

'Beginning at San Francisco,' Sheelagh could not help but say.

'That's right,' he gave her a hard, curious look. 'Why, something wrong with 'Frisco, nurse?'

'N-no,' Sheelagh said hurriedly, 'of course not, just a little excited, I guess. My . . . my two passengers, patients, whatever it is I have to think of them as, could you tell me what's wrong with them, please?'

'Certainly,' the traffic control officer looked at her for a long second, as though surprised at this sudden show of interest, then he gave a tiny shrug and consulted a typed list attached to a clip-board.

'Mrs Cassell suffers from what they've liste
here as nervous exhaustion.' He glanced at Shee
lagh and the suggestion of a smile touched hi
lips. 'Now that, I should imagine, might con
ceivably cover an enormous amount of ground
wouldn't you say, nurse? Especially when you ti
it in with the fact of Mrs Cassell being a multi
millionairess.'

Cassell. The name suddenly registered witl
Sheelagh. 'Mrs Anthony Cassell?' she asked.

'The same,' the control officer nodded. 'Th
widow of the big advertising man, the guy that wa
supposed to own a piece of practically every ac
agency in Madison Avenue.'

Now it was Sheelagh's turn to nod thought
fully. She remembered other things about An
thony Cassell now, snippets of news that alway
seemed to make the front pages of the nationa
news sheets. How his wife was famous for putting
on more temperamental turns than an over-
worked prima donna, especially in public. How
because of this, the husband had sought com-
parative peace in the arms of other women
something the news services were not slow tc
report on whenever some new scandal came tc
hand.

This, plus the fact that Mrs Cassell at every
opportunity cried out to the world what sort of **a**

eel she had married, had done nothing to help
long Cassell's career, and while he had still died
n immensely wealthy man, it had been rum-
ured, Sheelagh recalled, that his empire was, or
ad been, slowly crumbling because of lack of
aith in him as an individual, a public personality.

'Your other patient,' the control officer went
n, interrupting Sheelagh's musing, 'is a Mr
Kenneth Appleton.'

'And what is he suffering from?' Sheelagh
sked, beginning to wonder if in this new line of
work she would perhaps be collecting too many
poiled and neurotic people, unconsciously, then,
omparing them to the sort of patients she had
ursed in Community—the poor and suffering of
he world, people who had really needed her
rofessional services, to whom the attention of a
octor and nurse literally meant the difference of
fe and death. Well, Sheelagh thought wryly,
hat was what one got for taking on a glamour
ob. You couldn't have it both ways, the glamour
nd excitement plus the satisfaction of knowing
hat one's work is needed and appreciated. The
ontrol officer went on in reply to her question:

'He's just out of hospital for osteomyelitis.' He
aised a curious brow and looked up at Sheelagh.
That's something to do with the bones, isn't
?'

'That's right,' Sheelagh agreed, 'inflammation of the bone marrow. It used to be considered one of the worst diseases, now penicillin has revolutionised things. Does it say what part was affected? It usually attacks the long bones of the body, the arms and the legs.'

The officer consulted his sheet, then shook his head. 'Nope, just says convalescent period following osteomyelitis.'

'Well,' Sheelagh smiled and made a slight move towards the door, indicating that she was about through with her questions, 'they don't sound so bad. Thank you very much. Now if you'll excuse me, I'd best catch up with the others. I expect the skipper will want to get us organised.'

She hurried from the room before the man could reply. Although she was still extremely nervous about things, especially the prospect of going back to San Francisco, the information she had gathered on her two patient passengers had mollified her to a certain extent. She was used to handling neurotics, as she felt certain Mrs Anthony Cassell would turn out to be. In one of the wards she had worked in before graduating they had set up a special corner where the study of the women could be made, their effect upon one another gauged, whether it was a good thing

r a bad thing to put neurotics together, whether
hey fed on one another's particular neurosis or
whether, seeing the extreme behaviour of other
ndividuals, had a stabilising effect.

And as for the osteomyelitis case, that posed no
articular problems, either, for the man would
ot have been discharged from hospital had there
een any suggestion of danger or possible com-
lications.

heelagh had, she very soon discovered, been
worrying about nothing. The airline worked to a
plit-second time-table so far as personnel were
oncerned. Barely had they left the plane that had
erried them across from the capital than they
were filing up the gangway into the huge jet for
he pre-flight check-ups.

But Sheelagh's eyes had automatically worked
vertime as they circled the airport in an
ttempt to locate the hospital. She realised
with a start that her nose was pressed tightly
gainst the window as she stared down at
he panoramic view of the city that had been
er home for such a very long time. She also
ealised that she had been wondering—as she
earched for the hospital among the jumble of
he city—what Michael was doing at that moment. Whether he was on duty or not, whether

he was making his rounds or was perhaps in surgery, working alongside his beloved 'Wilky'.

And then they had been down, and the captain, a short, stubby man with a ready smile and shrewd blue eyes, was escorting her across the tarmac to the huge silver jet, chatting to her to put her at her ease.

His name was Bob Marlowe, and he had been a bomber pilot during the Vietnam War, had served a stint in Korea between working for the airline, flying transports.

'I think you'll be more than okay,' he said, smiling and nodding as he assisted Sheelagh through the exit hatch and into the long, elegant interior of the jet, with its mathematical rows of seats. 'Just remember there're eight of us, and all seven of your co-workers will be eager to help you along should you strike a rough patch, okay?'

'Fine,' Sheelagh smiled, liking the man immensely.

'I know this must be a little rugged for you,' he went on, leaning a hip against one of the seats and folding his arms, 'collecting us for your first flight. Personally, I think Personnel was wrong in detailing a new girl for this. But I expect you'll make me eat those words.'

'I'll try,' Sheelagh smiled again, beginning to

nwind under his friendly and reassuring manner
nd personality.

'I know you will,' he grinned. 'You've got a
undred and sixty-five passengers, remember,
ut there's one steward, Barney Elkington, as
ood a man as you'll find. And there're three of
ou stewardesses, so I think you'll find things
ill be more than okay.'

'Do I more or less concentrate on the two pati-
nt types?' Sheelagh asked, beginning to feel all
f her old fear and apprehension return now that
he had allowed herself to think of her re-
ponsibilities, 'or should I circulate, work with
he other girls?'

'I guess I'll leave that to you, Sheelagh. You'll
ave to determine how sick Mrs Cassell and Mr
ppleton are and more or less play it by ear,
kay?'

'Okay.'

'Fine. Well,' he started away down the corridor
f the jet towards the flight deck, 'I've got a
ouple of million things to check, so if we're ever
oing to make Paris I guess I'd best get started.
ee you, nurse!'

Sheelagh watched his bulky figure disappear
hrough the hatch and into the control area with a
nking heart, feeling terribly alone now that the
aptain's reassuring presence was gone, wonder-

ing just what it would be like, flying the polar
route, jetting above the most lonely, inhospitable
spot on the whole planet. Well, one thing was
sure, she was soon going to find out!

CHAPTER TEN

THEY had flown straight to Fairbanks, Alaska, and now they were passing over Barrow on their way across the Arctic Ocean. The four mighty engines screamed their power, as though defying the monsters that dwelt beyond the Arctic Circle to do their worst, that, at better than six hundred miles per hour—five hundred and twenty knots, to be strictly technical—they were safe from the demons of the ice and snow and unbelievably low temperatures that existed amidst the terrible desolation of the ice-caps.

The near-supersonic whine of the jets had long ago faded into the background of Sheelagh's conciousness, so that now the sound was a part of her, had merged into her mind, her thought-patterns, and she knew she would feel strange when they finally cut out, when she climbed down the ramp and on to solid ground once again.

Mrs Anthony Cassell had been all that Sheelagh had been expecting, and worse. In her early fifties, she was a large woman with a bloated face, baggy with dissatisfaction, and hard little eyes, which she made appear even harder by the use of heavy eye make-up, something that looked pathetically out of place on so old a woman. She fussed over herself as though she were the only person in the world, and it was quite clear from the outset that she expected Sheelagh, in fact every member of the cabin staff, to do the same. She spoke with an ugly mid-Western accent, as hard and brittle as were her tiny black eyes. In fact everything about her, from her voice to her flamboyant style in clothes, jarred on Sheelagh.

Mr Appleton, on the other hand, was charm itself. In his late fifties, he was a fatherly type with thick white hair and wise, understanding eyes. Quite obviously it had been his right leg which had been affected by the streptococcus germ, for he had used a stick to walk with, and now that he was sitting down he kept it stiffly out-thrust before him, supported on the heaped up pillows that Sheelagh had hastily provided.

'Hell of a thing,' he smiled up at Sheelagh as she came by to ask if there was anything she could get him, slapping his leg as he spoke. ' come down with one of those staph infections which I thought was bad enough—boils every where and a leg the size of a balloon—and then just as I think all the antibiotics and penicillin I'd been pumping into myself are clearing things whammo, I collect this little lot . . . doctor says was lucky not to have lost my leg.'

'You must have left it a long time before seek

ng medical aid, then,' Sheelagh said. 'Nowadays, surgical intervention is necessary only in a very small minority of cases. What happened, were you away somewhere, somewhere fairly remote?'

'You're a good guesser,' Appleton chuckled, grinning up at Sheelagh, 'either that or a darn good nurse. Yes, as a matter of fact, we were in Mexico—my son's going to be a geologist, and he invited us down to watch him doing a little field work. I suddenly came down with this fever, temperature of a hundred and four, and this hellishly painful leg ... so tender I could barely stand a sheet over it. The nearest doctor was miles away, so we intended to ignore it, watching it and hoping it would clear up, sort of thing.'

'You really were lucky,' Sheelagh nodded. 'If you do leave it alone, ignore it, almost invariably bone destruction sets in, what we call necrosis. Abscess formation takes place, and there's danger of an extension of the suppuration to neighbouring joints.'

'Or,' Appleton interrupted, smiling as he did so, 'general blood-poisoning may well result. Sorry to cut in on you, but my doctor gave me a lecture, too. I guess I know as much about osteomyelitis as you professionals.'

'Miss!' a man seated across the passageway to Appleton reached out and touched Sheelagh's arm, causing her to turn around quickly before she could reply to her patient. 'Sorry, but I think you might be wanted back there,' he indicated the seat three down from the rear of the cabin, the seat occupied by Mrs Anthony Cassell.

Sheelagh glanced back at the woman with annoyance, recognising the set expression of her patient and knowing that almost certainly she was going to start complaining about something or other—probably the lack of the attention she expected to receive. Uttering a hasty excuse to Appleton, she hurried back, stood politely beside the wealthy widow's seat.

'You wanted me, Mrs Cassell?' she asked quietly.

'I thought,' she said loudly, in a voice practically every one of the hundred and sixty-odd other passengers could hear, despite the howl of the jets, 'that I was supposed to have the services of a trained nurse!'

'You have, Mrs Cassell,' Sheelagh said in the same quiet voice, forcing herself to remain calm in the face of the coming tirade.

'How long did you do ... three months?' There was rudeness, sarcastic scorn in the widow's voice, and the dark eyes narrowed until they were little more than slits as she glared up at Sheelagh.

'I'm a fully-qualified R.N., Mrs Cassell. Now what is it that I can do for you?'

'I want to sleep. Get me something, pheno-barbitone. A full grain.'

Sheelagh hesitated. It was tempting, at least it would put the old so-and-so out to it for a few hours, leave her in comparative peace. But all of Sheelagh's nursing instincts, the ingrained ethics that went hand-in-hand with being a good nurse, rebelled at having a patient demand a certain medicine, even down to the dosage. The bar-biturates were excellent if used properly, as seda-tives in emergency, but a couple of aspirin would, in this instance, serve the same purpose.

'Would you allow me to get you something, Mrs Cassell, something not quite so drastic?'

'Now look!' Mrs Cassell—the neglected and despised wife of one of the country's top advertis-ing men, the woman who, in her way, had has-tened her husband's end by making his life a misery—slapped a beefy hand down on her knee and positively glared at Sheelagh. 'I'm a first-class passenger, and I paid extra for the services of a nurse because I'm a sick woman. Now I don't want *you* to tell me what's good for me and what isn't! I've been through hell.'

A whine of self-pity entered her voice, and watching her, Sheelagh saw the beady little eyes flick around to see what sort of an audience she had drummed up for herself. 'Nobody will ever know ... and now I'm sick because of it, *very* sick. So please,' she looked up at Sheelagh and the large, fleshy, sulky mouth stretched into an empty smile that was completely and utterly phoney, 'be a good girl and give me something to let me get a few hours' sleep. Let me stop thinking about it all for a little while.'

'Yes, Mrs Cassell.' Sheelagh inclined her head in a slight bow and walked back down to the rear of the plane and into the tiny pantry.

The steward, Barney Elkington, a slight little man with a mass of tight fair curls and laughing blue eyes, glanced at Sheelagh as she dropped the curtain behind her and stood leaning wearily against the wall.

'Hi! What is it ... they getting to you?'

'Only one of them,' Sheelagh managed to dredge up a brief smile, liking the steward, appreciating him for his bright and breezy manner, the kindness that she recognised in his eyes. 'Mrs Cassell.'

'Don't let her get you down.' He winked and put the final touches to a salad, placing skilfully sliced radishes and pieces of tomato on top of the celery and lettuce. 'Best way to treat her is smile and say "Yes, madam" all the time, kid her along, in other words.'

'You sound like you've collected her before.'

'Mrs Cassell? Heck, she's a regular, one of the "too-much brigade".'

'The which brigade?' Sheelagh frowned, not sure that she had heard right.

'It's what I call them,' Barney Elkington went on, grinning at Sheelagh's perplexity. 'The women—men, too—with more money than they know what to do with, who think the world's their oyster, who spend their lives flying round and around in search of a happiness they wouldn't recognise even if they met up with it face-to-face. Mrs Cassell's one of the top-ranking officers in the brigade in my book. She led her husband a dog's life from all that I hear. Now she's trying it on with everyone she comes into contact with, people unfortunate enough to have to be, to a degree, anyway, subordinate to her.'

'Like stewards and stewardesses,' Sheelagh suggested, smiling wryly.

'That's right,' Barney lifted the salad and held it aloft for Sheelagh to admire, as though it were a piece of fine art. 'How'd you like it? Mrs O'Callaghan ordered it . . . she's another of my "too-much brigade", one of the "not-too-bad" ones.'

'Only slightly neurotic, you mean,' Sheelagh smiled, wondering how anyone could want a salad flying over the North Pole, 'and if she's not happy with that, she really is sick. It's a work of art, Barney.'

'Thank you,' the steward gave a little bow. 'You're most kind, madame. And now if you'll let me out of this dox box, I'll see that Mrs O'Callaghan gets her vitamins.'

Grinning, Sheelagh edged to one side to allow him out of the pantry. She looked at the gently swinging curtain in thoughtful silence for some seconds after Barney had gone, listening to the steady whine of the jets, thinking about the icy whiteness below, over which they flew. Then she turned to the medicine cabinet, took down a bottle of phenobarbitone capsules, and shook out two—two half-grains. If Mrs Cassell wanted to sleep she would let her, Sheelagh decided, and she felt sure that even the medical superintendent himself, Alex Kerensky—were he present—would have agreed that with such a patient the treatment was more than justified.

There was, Sheelagh quickly came to realise, no excitement, no marvellous and colourful adventure to be enjoyed within the confines of a pressurised cabin. The long, cigar-shaped area could just as easily have been situated in the midst of a desert, or in somebody's back yard, instead of being hurled through the skies at six hundred miles per hour by the huge turbo-jets.

Because of the terrain over which they flew, or more specifically, because of the atmospheric conditions, there was absolutely nothing to be seen save a huge sea of tumbled white cloud. And there was nothing, Sheelagh decided after what seemed hours of gazing down at it, praying for a break in the canopy that so successfully hid the ground and the seas over which they flew, quite so boring or tedious to look at as a never-ending stretch of clouds.

She chatted with Mr Appleton, discovered that he was flying to Paris on business, and that he had three children, a boy and two girls, she talked with the lady up front from Appleton, learned that she was from Ohio and was spending her husband's insurance money on a round-the-world trip, the husband being too busy at the office to come along. And she learned that the man sitting behind Mrs Cassell had just got a divorce and would greatly appreciate the opportunity to show Sheelagh the sights of Paris.

As the boredom continued, the steady, relentless whine of the jets seeming to add to it, underline it, emphasise it, until Sheelagh felt that if it did not end soon she would scream. She could not help but compare it to the life she had been used to, the life that she really loved—that of nursing.

With affection, she recalled the nights when she had been run off her feet, when everything that could possibly go wrong did, the times when emergency sent up patients by the dozen, or when influenza virus knocked out a third of the staff, meaning double work for everybody. That was what she wanted, that was what she missed. The frantic activity of it all, the constant coming and going, the never-ending challenge to one's skill and initiative that the myriad different types of patients and illnesses presented.

And that, Sheelagh was to discover all too soon, was the pattern for women who flew the jet lines, the hostesses or stewardesses. What excitement there was they had to find among their passengers, which was probably why, Sheelagh decided ruefully, so many girls finished up marrying them . . . simply because there was nothing else to do but flirt.

The stop-overs were too brief to be anything else but that—stop-overs. So the closest that Sheelagh came to seeing Paris was the bird's eye view of the famous City of Light they had as they circled around before coming in to land, the brief glimpses of the Eiffel Tower, the Seine, the wide-spaced boulevards.

It could just as well have been an American city, New Orleans, or maybe her own San Francisco.

The split-second schedule never allowed them a moment's freedom, Sheelagh learned. No sooner had they touched down, it seemed, than they were off again on some other flight. Either that or they were sleeping the sleep of exhaustion in some foreign hotel or other, places that, for the most part, lacked even the most elementary plumbing and the other taken-for-granted aspects of modern twentieth-century comfort.

She had been with the airline, flying almost constantly, or so it seemed, for better than five weeks before Sheelagh became aware that certain official strings were being pulled by Terry in an effort to get her appointed to his plane.

With Washington as her headquarters, she had maintained the comfortable little apartment that Terry had found for her in Georgetown. She and the landlady, Mrs Newman, had become fast friends, so that it was just like returning home to let herself in through the front door and yell a cheery hello to the plump, kindly woman, surprising her with some knick-knack or other picked up in an overseas gift or curio shop.

Terry saw her when he could, but they were rather like a doctor and a nurse working in a large city hospital. Their hours of duty were usually different, which meant the opportunities for enjoying one another's free time were rare indeed.

And then one day Sheelagh's suspicion that Terry was up to something in regard to personnel appointments was heightened to downright certainty when Mrs Newman handed her two letters. One was a special delivery from San Francisco, the other the red and white envelope used by the airline for its correspondence. She had just completed a trans-Atlantic trip from the United Kingdom, a particularly fatiguing one.

Sheelagh, after thanking her landlady and tactfully refusing her offer of coffee and a snack, retired hurriedly to her room, kicking off her shoes and throwing herself down on to the bed, staring curiously at the two letters.

The one from 'Frisco, naturally, was the first to be read, and her heart was thumping madly as she hastily tore open the envelope. Who could it be from ... Michael? Had he swallowed his pride, overcome his Irish temper to the point of actually writing her?

Was it from Fitzy? The envelope had been typed, as was the letter, which tended to rule out both, although Fitzy might have borrowed a typewriter.

Dear Miss Landers, the letter said, *The airline for which you now work has approached us with a* request for further references regarding your work while employed at this hospital, and this we have done.

However, I would like to point out that this will be the last occasion on which we will feel at liberty to do this, it not being the policy of the hospital to issue more than one reference. We would appreciate it if you would kindly bear this in mind should you approach any future employers.

The letter was signed: *Corinne Huntley, Staff Supervisor (Women)*

Sheelagh re-read it, and felt like crying, hurt by the rude harshness of its tone, so typical of the woman herself. It was as though all the long hours of study she had put in, when she had somehow kept herself awake with black coffee in order to cram for a coming exam, all the countless occasions when she had worked through, putting in long and killing hours to help out, all of this and countless things more meant nothing to the people in charge, who ran the hospital.

Common sense, and because she knew so well the woman who had dictated the letter, forced Sheelagh to rise above her original hurt. She made herself realise that it was not the fault of the hospital, of people like Kerensky and Wilky—they were good men, but that it was purely one more bitchy action by the staff supervisor, Corinne Huntley.

But still, she thought savagely as she crumpled the letter into a tight ball and dropped it to the floor, it was not a very nice thing to receive, even if one did fully appreciate the sort of person behind it, whose work it was.

But why had the airline, the personnel people, approached the hospital in the first place? She had given them all the references they could possibly need when applying for the job. And why hadn't they said something to her about it before writing away?

Curious and angry together, Sheelagh slit open the second letter, from the head office of the air line, and started reading.

Dear Miss Landers, it began, *It is with pleasure that we are able to inform you that as from the first of next month you will be considered a fully-trained and experienced first stewardess and therefore will be paid accordingly.*

We would like to take this opportunity to say how happy we are with your work, and to venture the hope you will remain with us for a satisfactory time—from both our viewpoints.

Because of your excellent record, Captain H. E. Johns has requested that you be appointed to his team, and this we have agreed to. Will you, therefore, consider yourself under Captain Johns' command upon your return to duty.

Again our congratulations, and please find attached our cheque, your share of a recent staff bonus paid to all personnel.

The letter was signed, *E. S. Metcalf, Senior Manager (Personnel)*

Sheelagh opened the smaller envelope that was pinned behind the letter. Inside was a cheque for a hundred and thirty-five dollars, seventy-five cents.

She gazed down at it, smiling, amused by the exact amount, the implication of complete fairness, but smiling, too, because of the warmth the letter had contained, so very different from Corinne Huntley's effort.

Captain Harry Johns! Terry's skipper! Of course, it all made sense, he had been pulling strings, using his many contacts within the organisation of the airline, to work this thing, get her detailed to the same crew as himself.

Someone tapped at the door, disturbing the happy flow of Sheelagh's thoughts. Before she could even begin to think about calling out in reply, Mrs Newman's voice said: 'Sheelagh honey, sorry to worry you, I know you're beat, but there's a call for you . . . long-distance.'

Feeling that everything was happening to her at once, her heart skipping wildly, her mind filled with delightful anticipation as she tried to imagine who could possibly be calling long-distance, Sheelagh hurried to the door, thanked a beaming Mrs Newman, and ran downstairs to the telephone table in the hall. She settled on the tiny stool and scooped up the phone. 'Hullo? Sheelagh Landers speaking!'

'Hi! It's me!'

Sheelagh recognised Terry's voice, and was aware of a little stab of disappointment, for she had been secretly—or was it subconsciously?—hoping it would be Michael, that he had somehow tracked down her number.

'Sheelagh? You there?'

'Yes,' she said quickly, forcing herself to sound happy and jovial and excited to hear his voice. 'Yes, I'm here. How are you, Terry?'

'Fine, just fine. Did you get to hear the news? You're on my team now, kiddo. How'd you feel about that?'

'Yes,' Sheelagh tried without success to keep the flatness from her voice, attempted to sound madly thrilled at the wonderful news of her transfer to Captain Harry Johns' team. 'I've just finished reading the letters, as a matter of fact. Do I have to thank you for all of this, Terry?'

'You do.'

'Well . . . thank you.'

'Honey,' his voice, for the first time, sounded

vaguely troubled. 'Honey, is anything the matter?'

'No, of course not,' Sheelagh replied, giving a quick, nervous laugh. 'I'm just a little tired, I guess. It was sweet of you, Terry, I mean that. You know, somehow I suspected that something like this was going on, I sort of had the feeling, and I must confess, I've heard a few whispers.'

He chuckled. 'I'm afraid we work for a pretty big family, and like most big families and small towns, everybody knows everybody else's business.'

'So we're going to be flying together, huh?'

'It looks that way, kitten!'

Sheelagh took a deep breath and mentally crossed her fingers before she spoke again. A lot depended on the way in which Terry answered her, perhaps more than she cared to think about or admit to.

'And that means what, exactly,' she said finally, 'apart from the fact—or is it in addition to?—that we'll be members of the same team, crew-mates?'

'What would you like it to mean, Sheelagh?' Terry countered, his voice deep, serious, with all the earlier flippancy gone. 'It means, on the surface, at least, that we'll be working together, will be arriving at the same places at the same times, instead of my being in, say, Bangkok while you're maybe in London or Paris. I've told you the way I feel about you ... I haven't been keeping any secrets.'

'No,' Sheelagh admitted, feeling very much the heel, knowing that she was hurting him with her wary questions, the verbal fencing they suddenly seemed to be indulging in. 'No, you haven't, Terry.'

'You're not happy about it, is that it?'

There was anger in his voice, anger and disappointment and a deep-seated pain. Sheelagh looked down at her left hand, and was surprised to see that it was stiff as a claw, the fingers moving in nervous reflex, her nails scraping at the material of her dress.

Well, she'd started all this, she hadn't *had* to begin putting the poor guy through the third-degree. But she had wanted to get things finalised, had wanted to hear him repeat his claims on her, describe his love for her ... his desire for her. For suddenly it was tremendously important that she knew just where she was going.

The past few weeks had been trying, to put it mildly. She seemed to have been existing in a vortex, a crazy mix-up consisting of her basic love for nursing, for the hospital, and the kindness of the people around her and with whom she ow worked. And then, as if that were not enough, the deep and underlying problem of Michael and Terry.

Which of the two men *was* for her? Sheelagh thought desperately. Did a woman, any woman, really have a choice, or was it all left in the lap of the gods, so that it was decided elsewhere just when a certain man should appear at a certain place and time in a girl's life? Maybe that was it, Sheelagh thought, remembering all the girls she had known who had married on the rebound after a silly quarrel with the boy they really loved. They lost what, for them, could have been *the* big romance, grabbing instead the first man to happen along . . . probably ending up with three or four children who would be brought up in an atmosphere of eternal tension and bickering because their mother had made that one foolish mistake before they were born.

So how did you tell? she wondered. If a girl was too cautious she ended up on the shelf. By the same token, if she was too hasty in her choice it had every chance in the world of turning out badly, and a bad marriage was what Sheelagh feared above all else, because she was more than aware of the tremendous demands marriage made upon the individual, the price one paid *for* a mistake.

So where did that leave her, exactly? Probably she was on the right track in feeling Terry out again, substantiating his earlier claims and promises. Let him lay down his cards, and then she, Sheelagh Landers, would decide whether or not she should pick them up.

'Sheelagh? . . . honey, you still there?' his voice came in her ear, startling her, bringing her back to reality with a jolt.

'Yes, Terry, I'm still here.'

'You're very quiet.'

'I . . . I was thinking.'

'About what? How to give me the big brush-off without hurting my feelings too much?'

The anger, the disappointment had changed to bitterness now—a bitterness so great, so naked, it made Sheelagh wince. She took the phone from her ear and stared at it thoughtfully, wondering just what to say, wishing there was some way in which she could stretch time, the way some of the psychic-type drugs were supposed to do for their users, hallucinogens like LSD-25, psilocybin, and mescaline. It would be nice to have a full week in which to consider her reply, and then, when she had finally made up her mind, to find that Terry was still waiting on the other end of the line. Only unfortunately, Sheelagh thought with a sigh, bringing the phone back up to her ear, life wasn't even that easy.

'No, Terry,' she heard herself say in a tired
sort of voice that did not sound her own, 'don't
be silly. Why should I be thinking up a nasty thing
like that to say to you, especially after the way
you've helped me, your kindness?'

'Don't feel obligated in any way,' he replied,
coming close to snapping out the words. 'I don't
go for that "I-feel-sorry-for-the-poor-guy" stuff,
Sheelagh. If I've made a big idiot of myself now's
the time to say it. I've just not been seeing
enough of you, that's all. I've grown heartily sick
of you being on one side of the planet while I'm
flying around some place or the other. So I
pulled a few strings, asked a few people to pay
back favours owed. Now I'm not so damned sure
that I played it very smart! Kid, you'd better tell
me, you'd better level with me . . . have I been
sticking my neck out for no good reason?'

'Terry——' Sheelagh stiffened, her back growing
very straight. She took a deep breath and closed her
eyes, aware that her heart was pounding along at
trip-hammer speed, that the palms of her hands
had grown suddenly moist. 'Let's not rush
things—that, I think, is the best way right now.
You've never heard the full story behind my
wanting to get away from the hospital, from San
Francisco, but I expect you can guess. I need
time, Terry. I know that's something of a cliché,

137

but it happens to be the truth.'

'Okay,' he sounded very distant and aloof 'okay, Sheelagh, if that's the way you want it. I'll see you when you go back to duty. 'Bye now.'

He hung up.

Sheelagh looked at the phone for a long time before she finally moved her hand, replaced the instrument on its stand. Far from feeling free with the time she had requested granted her, she was aware of a terrible constriction, as though a solid steel fence were being erected around her mind and was relentlessly closing in on her consciousness.

Had she done the right thing? Should she have been more honest, have told Terry the way she knew she still felt about Michael Kelman? She hadn't offered him a thing, Sheelagh realised, hadn't even had the common politeness to enquire just where he had been calling her from!

ɪᴛ was as though Fate had finally taken pity on
er, Sheelagh thought when she awoke the next
norning after one of the worst nights she could
ver remember having spent. For shortly after
he had showered, and midway through prepar-
ɪg herself something to eat—although she had
ever felt less like breakfast in her life—there was
n urgent knocking on her door and Aileen Roder
ounced into the room. She looked absolutely
abulous in a dazzling cotton dress that seemed to
ave moulded itself to her superb figure. Aileen was
ɪ the highest of high spirits, her eyes flashing,
er mouth stretched wide in a permanent grin.

'News, darling . . . wonderful news, and I want
ou to be the very first to know about it!'

'Could you possibly manage to sit down and
lrink a cup of coffee while you tell me?' Sheelagh
sked, pushing her friend gently backwards until
he toppled over and down on to the bed. She
vas almost as happy to see the wild-living, fun-
oving Aileen as, apparently, Aileen was about
ife generally, for just looking at her happy and
xcited grin had chased most of Sheelagh's blues

away. 'I never could stand jack-in-the-box people!'
she added, thanking the kind fate that had sen
Aileen to her on this morning of all mornings . .
when she really needed cheering up.

'He did it!' Aileen grinned up at her. 'He reall'
and truly went and did it! Can you beat it! Heck
after this I believe in the theory of mind ove
matter, but whammo! Because, darling, *it works*
it honestly works!'

'Slow down!' Sheelagh chuckled, holding u|
her hand in a halting gesture, like a traffic cop, ir
an effort to get through Aileen's intense excite
ment and still the nervous flow long enough to make
some kind of sense out of it. 'Who did what, exactly
and whose mind worked over what matter?'

'Louis, of course!' Aileen replied, as though
Sheelagh should have known exactly what she
was talking about, 'and my mind. I sort of willed
him into it, I guess,' she added, smiling across a
the wall with a secretive, knowing look in her
eyes, as though she possessed the power over life
and death, could maybe even move mountains
should the idea occur to her. 'I just used to sit and
look at him.' Her eyes came away from studying the
wall and she smiled up at Sheelagh. 'I'd wish like hel
that he would propose . . . and then last night he
did just that. Out came the words . . . the very
words that I'd been trying to pop into his mind!'

'Louis!' Sheelagh gasped, not believing her ears. 'You're going to marry Louis Castellano?'

'Like me, huh!' Aileen laughed, giving Sheelagh a quick, man-to-man sort of wink. 'You just can't believe it, a handsome hunk of a man like that. And something else, darling, he's loaded, his family are *very* well-to-do. Now how about that, handsome enough to be a damned film star and filthy rich into the bargain?'

'Aileen, are you sure, sure it's what you really want?'

Even as she spoke, Sheelagh found herself comparing the smooth-mannered, beautifully-tailored Italian with her own hard-working, rugged-looking Mike Kelman, and she knew that she could never in a million years be happy with such a man.

'*Honey!*' Aileen's eyes became as big as saucers. 'Are you *kidding*!'

'Sorry,' Sheelagh shrugged and made a small, apologetic gesture with her hands. 'I guess it seems to have happened so quickly, I mean, just how long have you known him, anyway?'

'*Ages*, or so it seems,' Aileen made a little grimace and sighed. 'I guess not so long, really, to be truthful. Hell, a gal's just never around long enough in this job to *see* a guy, I'm usually away in Timbuktu or some other hellishly remote place

instead of being sensible and staying put here i
Washington with my ever-lovin'.'

'You're the one who wanted to be a stew
ardess,' Sheelagh reminded her.

'That was in the B.L. era, honey . . . Before Loui
Now I wish I were a humble typist working for
pittance in some government office or other.'

'Preferably close to the Italian Embassy, c
course,' Sheelagh said, grinning.

'But natch!' Aileen's brows soared, and onc
more her eyes became huge blue saucers. 'Well
aren't you going to congratulate me? I take th
trouble to dash over here, knowing you'd checke
in from a flight yesterday, because I wanted you t
be the first to hear my great news, and all you ca
do is shoot doubtful and morbid questions at m
like a pessimistic older relative!'

'Sorry!' Sheelagh laughed. 'Accept my sincer
apologies, will you, please . . . pretty please?'

'I'll think about it,' Aileen said, wrinkling he
nose. 'And now you can feed me some of tha
coffee you seem so anxious to get rid of. I'n
plumb talked out . . . right now all I want to do,
she gave a huge sigh and gazed fondly at her wall
'is sit here and dream about him. The lovable
handsome big ox!'

It was too nice a day to spend indoors, both girl

ecided, so after making a quick snack of poached gs, toast, and coffee, Sheelagh dressed and they ught a cab downtown.

It was a truly lovely day, Sheelagh thought as e gazed out of the car window at the graceful read of the Potomac, and for perhaps the undredth time she found herself appreciating e beautifully laid-out capital, with its wide, ee-lined avenues, the general air of spaci- usness. They passed the American University, e Corcoran Gallery of Art, and finally ordered e cab to stop just down from the Department of e Interior building. They walked, then, down d into the huge area of Potomac parks that sur- unded the Tidal Basin, so famous for its huge ng of Japanese cherry trees.

'Let's sit, huh?' Aileen stopped and pointed wn at the soft grass. They were directly oppo- te the Tidal Basin, the starkly white, monolithic ger of the Washington Monument reflected in e stretch of the water, its image rippled gently to d fro as lazy zephyrs of wind ruffled the surface.

The grass was as soft as it looked, and the sun as warm on Sheelagh's bare shoulders, for she d selected a plain red cotton off-the-shoulder ess that she had picked up for a song in Hong ong. But she knew that she did not match up to ileen, who had been the target for all male eyes since they had paid off the cab.

'Well, let's talk about you for a change,' Aileen said when they had discussed Louis Castellano at length, had examined him as husband-potential from every conceivable angle. 'I hear you're going to be changed around, that you'll be flying with Terry Fitzsimmons.'

She spoke casually, and her eyes seemed focused on the reflection of the monument in the water, yet Sheelagh felt that there was a tension, an eagerness to learn exactly what was going on, and then she remembered the way Aileen and Terry had clashed the night that Louis had taken them all to the wonderful Italian restaurant. Apparently it worked both ways, for Aileen had sounded more than passingly curt as she had uttered his name, had even seen fit to tack the surname on to the Terry.

'It gets around, doesn't it?' Sheelagh smiled as she spoke, although somehow she didn't feel very much like smiling. It was irritating to know that the world and his uncle knew everything about one's movements, sometimes, apparently, even before you knew yourself. 'Yes, Aileen, when I go back to duty I join Captain Johns' team.'

'And how do you feel about that, happy?'

Sheelagh looked at her friend closely. Aileen still kept her gaze fixed on the water, but Sheelagh could all but see the pricking of her ears as she waited for the reply to her seemingly casual question. 'I guess so,' she said at last, trying to sound non-committal, as though she hadn't spent all the previous night lying staring at the ceiling of her room, worrying about it. Whether she wanted to be 'on' with Terry Fitzsimmons or not; whether she loved Michael or not.

'He's pretty crazy about you, you know,' Aileen twisted slightly and Sheelagh collected the full force of her frank green eyes. 'I mean, for a guy to go to all *that* trouble to get his girl working with him!'

'You think he did, then, go to a lot of trouble, I mean?'

'But for sure, honey!' Aileen's voice registered her amazement that anyone working for the airline should *not* have heard of the complications behind the transfer. 'He doesn't rate all that high, you know, he's still very much a junior pilot compared to some of the guys flying for the line. I bet it cost him a heck of a lot of effort to get you detailed to Harry Johns' team.'

'I guess . . . I guess I didn't think of it in quite that way,' Sheelagh said softly, wondering just what the other girls would be thinking, the people who knew all about this effort of Terry's. Wondering, too, what they would say if she finally broke things off, if she did give Terry the polite brush-off as he had, in fact, seemed to half-way expect when he had rung her last night, especially when she had begun to talk evasively.

'Anyway,' Aileen came catlike to her feet, stood looking down at Sheelagh as she smoothed her rumpled dress down over her hips with her palms, 'you could do worse than Terry Fitzsimmons, honey. He's hellishly handsome in his way . . . if you like the tough and rugged type, and he's completely overboard for you, which is quite a combination for a girl to latch on to.'

'Providing, of course,' Sheelagh said, softly rising and standing in front of her friend, smiling to take any suggestion of sarcasm from her words as she brushed loose blades of grass from her dress and adjusted her neckline, 'the girl is overboard for the guy.'

Aileen did not reply or comment; she didn't have to. The knowledgeable expression in the depths of her eyes spoke volumes, suggested she more than understood the situation. Which, Sheelagh thought wryly as they began to walk slowly back through the park, was a lot more than she did.

Aileen had a date with Louis for two o'clock, which left Sheelagh somewhat up in the air for what remained of the day. Although Aileen insisted that she come along with them, Sheelagh had, naturally, vigorously refused, mainly because she sensed that, in her heart, Aileen was on tenterhooks in case she *had* said yes, had made it an awkward and probably embarrassing threesome instead of the sublime twosome Aileen was so obviously looking forward to. But, under pressure, Sheelagh had consented to share a hasty lunch with her friend before Aileen took off to meet her dream man.

They settled for the first restaurant they saw after leaving the park. Called, somewhat impressively, the Arval, it was large and elegant, was situated close to the Mall. It was, very obviously, a favourite lunching spot for the myriad civil servants who worked in the area, and Sheelagh could have sworn, as they were being shown through to a table, that she spotted a Senator or two among the well-dressed customers, something that made her feel very cosmopolitan and worldly.

They made small talk for a while, and then Aileen, as though by design, brought the subject of Terry up again. At first Sheelagh was tempted to be rude, to purposely and obviously ignore it, change the entire trend of the conversation, but before she knew it she was pouring her heart out, was telling Aileen everything that had happened—not only between Terry and herself, but also with Michael.

'Dr Michael Kelman,' Aileen said, savouring the name and looking away thoughtfully down the length of the restaurant, 'he sounds like quite a guy.'

'Yes,' Sheelagh admitted, feeling the old pangs of pain return, the long and empty longing to once again look into Michael's eyes, hear his wonderfully soft, lilting brogue. 'He's quite a guy, all right.'

'So what are you going to do about him, kid?' Aileen's gaze came back and settled on Sheelagh, her eyes probing her thoughts. 'Just let the whole thing die out, fade away?'

'He isn't ready for marriage yet . . . or me.' Sheelagh felt her cheeks begin to burn with the embarrassment of it as she replied. 'I don't think you should ever push a man . . . especially when he's made it so plain that he doesn't want to become trapped.'

'Who said anything about pushing?' Aileen demanded, her eyes wide in mock innocence. 'There's more than one way to skin a cat, my girl, which is a lousy simile, I know, but it gets my argument across. I believe in the old adage that anything worth having is worth going after, and quite obviously, darling, your little world revolves around this handsome Irish medic with a strong yen to become a surgeon.'

'But what can I do?' Sheelagh cried, beside herself with a mixture of embarrassment and frustration, for now that the problem of Michael was out in the open, as it were, she felt herself growing hysterical at the thought that there *might* just be a way back, that she could somehow get herself reinstated at the hospital despite her feud with Supervisor Corinne Huntley, might once again be able to call herself Dr Michael Kelman's girl.

For she knew now that she had been altogether too hasty in fleeing from a situation that had seemed both intolerable and impossible. She should have stayed put, waited for Michael to change his mind, weaken in his determination to allow nothing to stop him becoming one of the best surgeons in the country, because that, she knew, was what Aileen would have done. And she also knew that Aileen would have used every trick in the feminine book to attract Mike Kelman's attention, everything from creating a state of jealousy with a series of mild flirtations, to downright sexy and teasing behaviour that would pamper to the man in him.

'What can you do?' Aileen replied, a mischievous twinkle lighting her eyes. 'You can just leave it all to me, darling . . . to your clever, worldly-wise friend.'

And then Aileen absolutely refused to discuss the matter any further, dismissed the subject out of hand. The waitress came back with their order (they had both settled for a salad), apologised for having kept them waiting so long, explaining that the restaurant was terribly busy and was short-staffed into the bargain, and Aileen had an additional excuse for keeping the conversation away from the subject of Sheelagh and Michael and what she planned to do about their mutual problem. She was going to have to eat and run if she was ever going to be on time for her appointment with Louis.

And that was the way things were left—way up in the air, with a puzzled and vaguely frightened Sheelagh watching her friend run out through the restaurant on her way to keep her date with her wonder man. And yet somehow Sheelagh did not envy Aileen her happiness . . . especially not with Louis Castellano of the Italian Embassy.

CHAPTER TWELVE

CAPTAIN HARRY E. JOHNS, Sheelagh's new boss, was fortyish and fatherly, with iron-grey hair and iron-grey eyes, a strong chin and a humorous mouth. He was a tall man, though not as tall as Terry, and his figure was the figure of a man who kept himself in top physical shape, with wide shoulders, tapered waist, and the rolling, impressive walk of a Robert Mitchum.

Their jet was scheduled for the Rome–Athens run, calling first at New York, then across the North Atlantic, flying as the crow flies—straight to Rome, and then on to Athens.

Sheelagh, who had made the trip once or twice before when she had been attached to Bob Marlowe's crew, knew that they could expect quite a few Italians and Greeks among the passengers, many of them first-generation Americans, making the almost traditional trip back to the old country.

She had enjoyed their company on the previous trips, for they had been filled with good spirits at the prospect of going back home, of meeting up with members of their families. They had laughed and joked and sung their warm and colourful songs, so that she had been reminded of the night Louis Castellano had taken them to the Italian restaurant, for the atmosphere within the pressurised cabin of the huge jet had, for a short space of time, been almost identical to that memorable night.

'Glad you've joined us, Sheelagh,' Johns said as they walked across the tarmac towards the giant silver jet, 'glad Terry talked us into letting you transfer.'

'Where is Terry?' Sheelagh asked, nervous at the thought of having to face Terry, whom she hadn't seen for what seemed an age. She glanced around her at the rest of the crew—navigator, engineer, wireless operator, the steward and her fellow stewardesses to check that he *wasn't* included in the small group.

'Already aboard,' Johns nodded towards the nose of the jet, 'making the pre-flight check. But I was saying how glad I am you've joined us,' he went on a trifle impatiently, as though annoyed at the interruption, 'especially on this flight, because we've a passenger greatly in need of the services of someone like yourself.'

'Oh!' Sheelagh raised surprised brows. They had not mentioned it at the briefing; this was the first she'd heard that one of her charges was sick. Captain Johns went on:

'Little gentleman by the name of Leo Lazzeris. He's ten years of age, and is travelling alone.'

'And exactly what is it that's wrong with him, Captain?' Sheelagh asked. They had stopped just short of the ramp, and had continued talking while the other members of the crew filed up and into the plane. Purposely, Sheelagh kept her face towards the tail of it, afraid that perhaps Terry would be watching her from the windows of the flight deck, putting off the dreaded moment of meeting him as long as possible.

'Well, I'm no medic,' the Captain grinned, 'all I know is it's something to do with his back, his spine. I believe he was recently operated on for it.'

'And he's travelling *alone*?' Sheelagh was both shocked and incredulous, for usually any operation to do with the spine and the spinal canal was serious, and it was a horrifying thought that someone so young should have been left entirely to the care of strangers. Perhaps, as Johns had said, it *was* fortunate that she had joined his team, at least so far as little Leo Lazzeris was concerned.

'His grandfather wants to see him,' Johns explained, glancing hintingly at the open doorway. 'Apparently there was no one available to escort him.'

'Well,' Sheelagh, taking the hint, aware that the captain felt he had wasted enough time chatting, moved towards the ramp, 'we'll just have to do what we can for him, I guess. Thank you for your kindness, Captain. I hope I'll prove satisfactory to you. You know I'll be doing my best.'

'Can't ask for more,' Johns said cheerfully, swinging up on to the ramp and following Sheelagh into the plane. 'And don't forget, if you get any problems . . . yell. And the name's Harry, not Captain Johns.'

Once more the whisper of the jet was a lullaby, a background against which Sheelagh lived and worked. As she had expected, and as the names on the flight list had suggested, a good fifty per cent of her passengers were either Italian or Greek, with the bulk of them coming aboard in New York.

About two hours after leaving the coast behind them, when the U.S. was no more than a vague blackness on the edge of the visible horizon, and with the ocean looking as flat and hard as a giant airport runway were it not for the corrugations of the waves, waves that, Sheelagh knew, were, in reality anything from six to twenty feet in height. Terry came through the door of the flight deck, his head bowed to stop his cap from grazing the ceiling of the cabin. He nodded to one or two of the passengers as he passed, smiled at others, winked at a couple of small children. Then he was beside Sheelagh, his hand gripping her arm forcibly, guiding her back and into the pantry.

'D'you mind, Vince?' he asked Vincent Tasker, a slim young man with a degree in economics from Yale who, or so he claimed, was only working for the airline as a steward because it was the cheapest and fastest way to see the world. 'Just for a minute, huh? It's a little personal . . . okay?'

'Sure!' Tasker grinned knowingly at Sheelagh, winked at Terry, and left them alone.

'Hi!' Terry said the second he had gone, slipping his arms around Sheelagh's waist and pulling her gently to him. 'Long time no see! Last time we talked to one another we parted in an atmosphere of tension, as I remember, something for which I'd like very much to apologise about.'

'No apologies necessary, Terry,' Sheelagh replied, wondering how she could possibly slip out of his embrace without hurting his feelings. 'And incidentally, just where the heck *were* you calling me from?'

He gave a crooked grin and winked. 'Three guesses, and I guarantee you'll never make it.'

'It's a big world down there,' Sheelagh nodded down towards the floor, the gesture implying the spread of the earth beneath the jet's huge wings, 'it would take a lot more than three guesses, Terry.'

'You give up easy, don't you?' he grinned
'Okay, I was calling you from 'Frisco.'

Sheelagh stared up at him, her body stiffening
as the shock-words registered, ''Frisco?' she
echoed in a tight, strained little voice that did no
belong to her. 'You—you were there?'

'I'm often there, kitten . . . in your lil' ol' home
town. Matter of fact, I made it my business to
take a drive around to the hospital . . . I have a
sister there, remember? By the way, she sends
you her love . . . Fitzy says she misses you terribly and it's about time you wrote her.'

'You . . . you went to the hospital?' Sheelagh
repeated, still feeling as though she were in some
kind of shock-induced trance.

'That's what the man said!' Terry said easily,
grinning, his eyes roaming over Sheelagh's face,
searching it, recognising the shocked surprise in
her expression. 'You know how it is, kid, how
you get curious about people you happen to like
. . . or love. I guess I wanted to find out about
you, meet up with your friends, and of course, I
wanted to see my sister. Fitzy and I don't see half
enough of one another.'

Sheelagh jerked away from him, backing until
her shoulders were pressed against the cabin wall.
'Terry, you had no right to do that, to go snooping around behind my back!' She was angry, red-

rish mad, in fact, an emotion she seldom indulged in, that she normally kept under tight control. She was so angry, in fact, it took her all her time to stop from slapping Terry's face.

'I wasn't snooping,' he said evenly, leaning one broad shoulder against the door jamb, his piercing blue eyes meeting her angry gaze calmly. 'I happened to be in 'Frisco and I also happen to love you, or hadn't you heard?' he added, the sarcasm in his voice making Sheelagh wince, containing, as it did, so much of the pain that she herself felt whenever her thoughts reverted back to Michael and the hospital. 'I want to marry you, Sheelagh, I want to make you a housewife and a mother, or is that something pretty terrible in your book, not what you want, at least not with me?'

'Terry!' Sheelagh lifted her shoulders helplessly, shaking her head. 'Terry, please, don't make it harder than it already is.'

She hated herself at that moment. All the anger had evaporated, and she could feel only pity—and shame. Terry moved slowly forward, his hands reaching out for her. His lips were parted and Sheelagh could hear his breathing—long and heavy, the sound rising above the whispering jets. His hands touched her waist, slid around her, and once again he was drawing her slowly, relentlessly, towards him. And then his mouth was covering her own, and his lips were hard and demanding, bruising her own.

Sheelagh did not fight back, did not attempt to resist. She closed her eyes and waited until he grew tired of trying to get some kind of response from her. Finally he drew back, an expression of disgust on his face as he looked down at her.

'Sorry! I guess I made a mistake!'

'I'm sorry, Terry,' Sheelagh spoke in a low quiet voice, looking at him with a compassion, and understanding she had never felt before. She knew what it was to love and be rejected, and she would have given anything to have spared him but there was nothing else she could do. There was simply no alternative attitude to be adopted. And maybe, Sheelagh thought as she continued to look up into his face, maybe it was better this way.

'Yeah . . .' he backed away, wiping at his mouth with the back of his hand. 'Sorry! It's Michael, huh?'

'Yes,' Sheelagh nodded quickly, feeling a stab of pain in the region of her heart as she heard Mike's name mentioned.

'Well, I guess I'm losing out to a good man,' he said ruefully, pulling a handkerchief from his pocket and wiped lipstick from his mouth. He glanced down at the red smear that marred the handkerchief's whiteness, then up and across at Sheelagh.

'Because you see,' he went on, speaking in a low, flat sort of voice that concealed, Sheelagh knew, his pain, 'I also made it my business to seek out your Dr Michael Kelman . . . he's quite a guy, Sheelagh.'

Sheelagh could only stand and stare back at him, meet the gaze of the dark blue eyes, shadowed and deep now as they mirrored his hurt and pain. The two men in her life had met up, then, had, it was to be assumed, judged and appraised one another. Had Michael realised that he had been talking to a potential rival? Had Terry dropped any kind of hint? How had he gone about it, meeting Mike? Would Fitzy have introduced them, knowing the way her brother felt about her? Sheelagh wondered. Or would she have thought her loyalty belonged to her erstwhile room-mate?

As though reading her mind, Terry added: 'Don't worry, I didn't let the guy know that I'm in love with you. So far as Dr Kelman is concerned, I'm just Fitzy's brother. But I was curious to see him, I *had* to see him, in fact. Can you understand that, Sheelagh?'

'Yes,' Sheelagh nodded slowly. She *could*

understand, for she knew that had there been another woman involved when she had broken with Mike she would have been terribly curious to see her, would have experienced the same compulsion that Terry had shown in seeking Michael out. You knew that it would hurt, that it would only twist the knife in the wound, but you still felt forced to see the person who had stolen your happiness.

'Tell me,' she added, feeling her heart pounding madly within her, knowing that the adrenalin was racing through her bloodstream as tension and excitement built, was creating all the physical manifestations that accompany an extreme emotional state, 'Michael . . . how is he?'

Terry hesitated for a long second before replying, looking down at Sheelagh thoughtfully, weighing his words. Finally he asked: 'You want the truth, Sheelagh?'

Sheelagh closed her eyes and clasped her hands to her breast. *Did* she want the truth? Wasn't it, perhaps, better to leave some things alone, better not to torture oneself any further? Yet, even as the small bells of caution tolled their urgent message of warning, Sheelagh realised that she had to know, that every atom of her being demanded news of the man she knew she loved.

'Yes,' she said at last, opening her eyes and

looking up at Terry steadily, pretending a calmness that was completely counterfeit, 'yes, please tell me, Terry . . . how is he?'

'He's the saddest-looking guy I ever laid my eyes on. I guess I'm really cutting my own throat to say it, but it's the truth, and the truth was what you said you wanted.'

Sheelagh felt her world collapsing around her. Had there been any kind of an emergency, had the aircraft suddenly burst into flames or had all four engines suddenly stopped, she would not have been able to move. For a crazy, improbable second, it was as though Michael was standing in front of her, as though she was once again back in the hospital, assisting as instrument nurse at an op, watching with proud and loving eyes as Michael's skilful surgeon's hands worked to save the life of a patient.

'Sheelagh . . . honey? You all right?'

She felt Terry's hands grip her arm above the elbow, felt herself being gently but firmly shaken. She shook her head violently, forcing herself to regain control. 'Y-yes,' she managed to get out, 'I—I'm okay.'

'You've gone white as a sheet! I guess you *really* love that surgeon of yours, huh?'

'I . . .' Sheelagh gave a wan little smile, 'I'm afraid so, Terry.'

'That,' he let go of her arms and stood back, and Sheelagh, looking up at him, had never seen such misery on a face before, 'just about lets me out, I guess. It's time to get off the train, as the wise man said, and I guess it's more than past the time that I began wising up to myself. So long, Sheelagh,' he touched long tanned fingers to the peak of his cap and smiled a thin, empty smile. 'I'll make my exit now, and I might as well play it corny all the way and say that you know that if there's anything I can ever do, if you ever need a friend . . . they call me Terry Fitzsimmons.'

And then he was gone, and there was only the whisper of the jets, the murmur of conversation from the huge passenger's cabin, and the great tearing cries that came bursting up through Sheelagh's chest, that exploded from her in a paroxysm of sobbing.

It was the steward, Vince Tasker, who walked in on the scene, who hurried into the tiny pantry and slipped a consoling arm around Sheelagh's quivering shoulders, murmuring kindly platitudes, frowning down at Sheelagh's tear-ruined face as she forced herself to look up at him.

He didn't demand an explanation, didn't utter a word, other than to tell Sheelagh that it was

kay, that everything was going to be all right, to
ry and take a pull on herself.

The gentle therapy worked, finally. Sheelagh
lipped away from him, feeling a complete and
tter idiot, dabbing at her face with her handker-
hief and wondering just what the steward must
e thinking about her disgraceful performance.
Luckily, by the greatest of good fortune, the
ther stewardesses had all kept out in the cabin,
hatting to and assisting the passengers, so that
he was granted the privacy she needed to get a
rip on herself, for even in the midst of her sob-
ing, Sheelagh had been worried that one of the
ther girls would decide to come into the pantry
or something or other. And women, she knew,
vould never be so understanding as men, would
ot be able to resist spreading the word around
hat Sheelagh Landers was crying her heart out.

'If you like,' Vince Tasker said quietly when
Sheelagh had at last mastered herself, was work-
ng on her face, attempting to do something
bout the red and swollen eyes, the shiny nose,
he trembling lips, 'I'll tell the skipper you're not
vell. There's an extra seat right aft that we keep
or an emergency such as this, for a passenger or
rew member suddenly taken ill. Why don't you
ry and take a little nap? Things won't look half
o bad afterwards.'

'I . . . I'll be all right, it's very, very sweet of you, but I'd prefer to work through this. I'm over it now, anyway.'

The steward did not attempt to argue with her or persuade Sheelagh otherwise; he merely nodded and smiled. 'Okay, if that's the case, how about a cup of java? Steaming hot, very sweet and with a huge spoonful of cream? I'm told hot sweet coffee is good for countering emotional shock.'

'You're an angel,' Sheelagh smiled at him with genuine fondness and appreciation. 'I'd love one!'

'Coming up!' The steward turned and busied himself with the percolator and cups and saucers. 'Leave it all to ol' Uncle Vince, Sheelagh, my girl. All *you've* got to worry about is making yourself look pretty again.'

Sheelagh smiled at his back, watching him pour and mix two coffees, grateful beyond measure for his kindliness. Make herself look pretty again! she thought as she once again studied her face in the mirror of her compact. Some task! She felt a hundred years old . . . she would *never* be pretty again! She didn't deserve to be pretty. Someone who had treated a swell guy like Terry the way she had!

CHAPTER THIRTEEN

THEY were some six hundred miles from the Portuguese coast, with the Azores four to five hundred miles astern of them, when little Leo Lazzeris first began to scream.

Sheelagh, following Captain Johns' sketchy briefing of the boy's condition, had attempted to acquaint herself with his case-history, but the lad carried no papers, and her attempts to talk to him, become friendly, had been met by a stony barrier of silence. The best she had been able to get from him were monosyllabic grunts—a mere yes or no—to her questions. Finally, exasperated, Sheelagh had given it up, putting it down to a mixture of shyness and fright or intense nervousness at the thought of jetting across the Atlantic alone—something for which, in all honesty, she couldn't blame him, for it was quite an ordeal for a ten-year-old.

One of the other stewardesses, a shapely blonde from the Mid-West named Dale Batten, was first to reach the boy, and Sheelagh quickly joined her, dropping the tray she was preparing and hurrying down the long corridor between the seats. The third stewardess, Maggie Cohane, after checking that the boy was really in a bad way, went through into the flight deck to inform Johns of the emergency.

Sheelagh made a cursory examination while Dale Batten did her best to quieten the boy, at the same time assuring the other passengers that everything was all right, and would they please not crowd around but kindly return to their seats.

Sheelagh did not like what she saw. There was acute dilation of the boy's stomach, and his temperature was unhealthily low, while his pulse was quick and shallow, fluttering along with the off-beat rhythm that was always associated with a major physical disturbance.

'Dale,' she looked up at the other stewardess, 'could you get me the medical kit? He'll have to be quietened down. I'm going to give him a jolt of morphine.'

'Right away!' Dale Batten vanished.

Captain Johns, his eyes worried, his mouth grim, hurried down the aisle and hunkered down beside Sheelagh as she continued her examination of the young passenger. 'What do you think?' he asked in a low voice, frowning as he spoke to signal that Sheelagh, too, should keep her reply confidential.

'I'd be able to answer that if I knew something about him,' Sheelagh said. 'This is madness, allowing a child of this age to travel alone after undergoing what I'm beginning to suspect was a major operation.'

'I agree,' Johns nodded grimly, watching the boy as he struggled to escape Sheelagh's tight restraining grip that was keeping him pinned down in his seat. 'But Italians have very strongly developed family ties, trees, whatever you like to call it. They tend to ignore common sense when family is concerned, and I can only suppose that something like that happened here. The boy's grandfather demanded to see him and the family did not, or could not, refuse. Even though the kid was fresh out of hospital. I know it sounds crazy, but you must have struck something along similar lines in your nursing.'

'Yes,' Sheelagh nodded, remembering the dozens of times they had lost emergency patients, some of them very seriously injured, people who had suddenly taken it into their heads to run off into the night. She could even remember a case where a male patient had got out of bed and gone home to his family for his Christmas dinner the day after an appendectomy. 'I guess I know what you mean.'

Dale Batten came back then with the medical kit, and Sheelagh quickly administered a shot of morphine intravenously, stood watching with a feeling of satisfaction and relief as the drug took effect, as the tiny figure slumped down into unconsciousness.

'He'll be out to it until we reach Rome,' she turned to the captain, 'but we'd better radio ahead, make sure that there's an ambulance waiting at the airport when we touch down.'

'Maggie,' Johns turned to the third stewardess, 'you heard that. Tell Hank to get it out immediately. Tell them all we know about the patient—age, recent spinal operation, no details available, but was in extreme pain and morphine was administered at,' he glanced at his wrist watch, 'fifteen hundred and thirty hours.'

'Right away!' Maggie hurried back along the aisle to the flight deck.

'Can we move him?' Johns asked, slowly coming to his feet. 'I'd like to take him right aft where it's a little more private.'

'All right,' Sheelagh looked down at the boy and nodded. 'It can't do any further harm under the circumstances, and I agree that he should have privacy,' she uttered the last sentence in a fairly loud tone, staring around at the wall of gaping, curious faces, annoyed to the point of being furious, at their morbid curiosity.

Later, when the boy was lying on the seat reserved for emergencies—the seat Vince Tasker had tried to talk Sheelagh into using—she made another, more thorough examination of her patient.

'Well?' Johns, who had been standing watching Sheelagh, asked when she finally came erect after covering the boy with a blanket, 'what's the verdict?'

'There's a very recent scar above the twelfth and thirteenth vertebrae.' Sheelagh did not attempt to keep the disgust from her voice as she spoke. 'They opened unilaterally.'

'And what does all that mean?'

'He was operated on for a laminectomy, the purpose of which is to expose the spinal cord and meninges, the entire spinothalmic tract.'

'I see!' the captain frowned down at the tiny, silent form beneath the blankets. 'That sounds pretty damn serious ... exactly what would it have been for—the operation, I mean?'

Sheelagh shrugged, and once again her voice was filled with bitterness and disgust—that anyone could have been so utterly callous as to allow a boy in such a condition to fly the Atlantic alone. 'Laminectomy's performed for several conditions, injury to the spinal cord and the vertebrae, inflammatory lesions, especially tuberculosis, tumours of the spinal cord and meninges.

'Without any sort of case-history to work with it's impossible to say. The boy will have to be thoroughly examined, I'm afraid.'

'Well, thanks!' the captain's voice was warm and grateful as were his eyes as he reached out and took Sheelagh's hand, gripped it tightly. 'As I said before we came aboard, I'm very glad you've joined us, Sheelagh!'

Sheelagh turned away, knowing that she was blushing, thrilled by the sincere compliment. It helped, in a small way, at least, to compensate for her earlier upset over Terry.

The four powerful jet engines continued to howl, thrusting them ever nearer to Rome.

The happy, jovial atmosphere that Sheelagh had expected from their passengers was nowhere apparent. The incident with little Leo Lazzeris had left everybody feeling low and dejected, and more than one woman was in tears as the tiny, blanket-covered shape was carried from the aircraft to the waiting ambulance, there to be fussed and cried over by a small, elderly man who was, quite obviously, the boy's grandfather, the relative Leo Lazzeris had been coming out to see.

'You did a very wonderful job, miss,' one of the women passengers said to Sheelagh as they stood together on the tarmac watching the pathetic drama. 'We're all very lucky that they employ girls like you on the planes ... thank you!'

Sheelagh, strangely touched by the sincerity of the woman, could only nod and smile. She was about forty-five, with a dark complexion and kind brown eyes, and she had a large mole low down on her left cheek near her mouth. She had no accent, but Sheelagh knew, without being told, that she was Italian.

It was things like that, she thought as they began getting ready for take-off, that made everything seem worthwhile, that made life a little easier, gave it some kind of meaning.

It was the sort of incident one met up with perhaps a dozen times a day in a large hospital. Yet for Sheelagh, a jet nurse, it came as an isolated incident that would not, she knew, be repeated for perhaps twelve months. And it was that thought, that sudden and abrupt realisation of things, that signalled the end of an era for Sheelagh, that finally crystallised her vague decisions to leave the airline and return to hospital work, that made her sit down and write out her resignation while the jet carried her on towards their ultimate destination—Athens.

She was back in Washington, waiting to receive an official reply to her letter of resignation, although she had been told verbally that it had been accepted.

Nobody had been happy about it. Harry Johns
had spent over three hours with Sheelagh trying
to persuade her to change her mind, to stay with
his team, and the staff people had been nearly as
persistent. Terry, of course, had kept his own
counsel, had not bothered to contact Sheelagh,
although she knew that he was hurt at the
thought of her quitting after he had worked so
hard on her behalf.

She had toyed with the idea of ringing him, or
at least writing to him, but had decided against it.
There would be time for that when she was back
in 'Frisco. It might only awaken something she
hoped was dead, might give him a resurgence of
hope, and that, Sheelagh knew, would only be
painful and embarrassing for both of them.

She was waiting for Aileen. She had just got in
from the London, Gander, Boston flight, and had
rung Sheelagh to say she would be over just as
soon as she'd told Louis she still loved him, had
showered and changed into something a little
more elegant than her uniform.

She arrived shortly after five, looking very sophisticated in a Paris-made suit, black and white
accessories, that she had been crazy to surprise
Louis with ever since she had bought it.

'Darling!' she gave Sheelagh a quick peck on
the cheek and fell on to the bed, kicking off her

tilt heels and lying back with a sigh, her nylon-clad legs crossed, one foot swinging. 'I'm beat! Completely! The worst bunch of passengers ever, and last week I collected a couple of conventions, and you know what *they're* like! But this crowd . . yikes!'

Sheelagh grinned at her and flicked on the jug for coffee. She knew Aileen. This worldly, madly sophisticated act of hers was a prelude to more serious matters . . . like why Sheelagh had re-signed from the airline.

'And how was Louis?' she asked while she waited for Aileen to get through with her little warm-up act. 'As handsome as ever?'

'Divinely so. He wants us to get married in Italy, isn't that romantic? His family own a villa on Ischia. Ever been there? It's next door to Capri and slap-bang opposite Naples.'

'I've flown over it,' Sheelagh laughed, 'which is about all you've done, isn't it?'

'I guess so,' Aileen admitted, losing a little of her sangfroid. 'I'm told it's a very beautiful little island, though. Louis raves over it.'

'Would you like anything to eat?' Sheelagh wanted to get off the subject of Louis, wanted to get around to the main subject of conversation and Aileen's real reason for calling on her—her resignation from the airline.

'What have you got? I'm not madly hungry, but I could nibble my way through a biscuit, I guess.'

'How about liverwurst sandwiches? I just bought a tin and the bread's fresh today.'

'You sold me!'

Sheelagh began making the sandwiches, spreading the paste on thickly, cutting the bread into neat little triangles that she arranged on a plate, then shredding a little lettuce to provide decoration. Aileen proved to be hungrier than she had claimed, for she got through two-thirds of the sandwiches before she even started to think about taking a sip of coffee.

'Now let's talk about why you *really* took time out from Louis to come and bat the breeze with me, shall we?' Sheelagh asked when they had finished the sandwiches, and were midway through their second cup of coffee.

'You mean your resignation, darling?' Aileen asked, her eyes widening in mock surprise. 'Honey, that's the *last* thing I want to talk about. Personally, I think you're doing a very wise and clever thing. Your heart was never really in this racket, anyway, you know it and I know it.'

Sheelagh laughingly agreed that they had both been right on that particular score. Aileen went on:

'So, having settled that question, shall we pass on to why I'm *really here*, why I *really* took time out from Louis to come and bat the breeze, as you put it?'

Before Sheelagh could reply, she went on: 'Remember I told you to leave everything to me regarding your big thing on one, Dr Michael Kelman? Well, anyway, *that's* why I'm here, kiddo . . . because I've got big news for you!'

'News?' Sheelagh came very close to dropping her cup. 'About Michael?'

'And who else are we talking about?'

'What . . . how? I mean . . .' Sheelagh was so flustered and nervous that her tongue absolutely refused to co-operate with her wildly spinning thoughts, the wishful half-dreams that flooded her mind like phantoms, so that she uttered empty and completely pointless words.

'Honey!' Aileen shook her head and clucked her tongue. 'You're really upset, aren't you? I knew you carried a torch for the guy, but heck, you don't have to go completely to pieces!'

'Aileen,' Sheelagh hurriedly put down her cup and saucer and turned to face her friend, 'please don't fool around. Just what is it you've done, what's this big news you're talking about?'

'He wants to see you . . . he knows that you've quit the airline. When I told him how you felt about nursing, how you'd missed terribly every darn thing that has to do with a hospital, especially,' Aileen's eyes sparkled with sudden mischief, 'a certain handsome young Irish surgeon ... Well, he just made me promise to talk you into catching the very next plane back to 'Frisco.'

'But ... but,' Sheelagh shook her head, her thoughts scattering every way like leaves before a fall wind, 'I don't understand. How did you get to see him, speak to him?'

'There are such things as telephones, you know,' Aileen quipped roguishly. 'I simply rang the hospital and asked for Dr Michael Kelman, and hey presto! there we were talking to one another!'

'Aileen, honestly!' Sheelagh did not know whether to be sore or happy, appreciative or angry.

'You don't like the idea, perhaps?' Aileen's eyes were twinkling and her lips were stretched wide in a grin. 'You'd have preferred for me to mind my own business?'

'No, of course not!' Sheelagh found herself beginning to grin, too. 'Thanks a bunch, honey, I really mean that, you're a real friend. Now tell me all about it. How did he sound? Was he surprised? Did he want to know how I was? Tell me all about it, right from the very beginning, when he first said hello.'

Laughing, shaking her head, her eyes twinkling merrily, Aileen settled comfortably back against the pillow and began her story of the long-distance call to the hospital, to Michael Kelman, M.D. . . . person-to-person.

CHAPTER FOURTEEN

THINGS happened so swiftly that Sheelagh had
the utmost difficulty in keeping in touch with
reality, for her mind, every conscious fibre in her
body, demanded that she indulge in long sessions
of day-dreaming, the subject being, of course,
Michael Kelman.

The letter from the airline arrived, officially
accepting her resignation, and included in it was
the balance of wages due to her. Aileen and Louis
threw her a farewell dinner party, and for the
sake of old times they visited the Italian restaurant Sheelagh had last been to with Terry, when
they had made a foursome, although, from the
way she was greeted by the regulars when they
arrived, it was obvious that Aileen had been
making rather a habit of the place.

Mrs Newman, Sheelagh's landlady, had a little
cry when she learned that she was to lose her
favourite, and for a change she gave Sheelagh a
little gift, a lovely pair of gold-and-opal earrings
that somehow managed to match exactly the
colour of Sheelagh's eyes.

Aileen and Louis presented her with a watch, a

strong, reliable nurse's watch, anti-magnetic, guaranteed for five years, and waterproof into the bargain.

They were all at the airport to see her off, and Sheelagh was crying unashamedly as she accepted the gifts. So far there had been no sign or word from Terry, something for which Sheelagh was extremely grateful, for she still suffered pangs of conscience when she thought of the way in which she had treated him, the way she had returned his kindness.

And then, scant seconds before departure time, a familiar figure came hurrying across to where their tiny group stood. The tall man, with wide, athletic shoulders and the rolling walk of a Robert Mitchum. Captain Harry Johns.

'Hi!' his strong, good-humoured features cracked wide in a grin. 'Thought I'd missed you. We just got in from the Lisbon run, they told us you were leaving Washington today, going back to 'Frisco.'

'Hello, Harry!' Sheelagh beamed at him, dabbing at her eyes, proud and thrilled that the skipper of the little team of which she had once been a member should have gone to so much trouble, and then, remembering her manners, hastily making the introductions.

'May I have a moment alone with her?' Johns

asked the others when the introductions were over, 'With the best little stewardess I've ever had?' Then, without waiting for any sort of reply, he took Sheelagh by the arm and steered her out of earshot of the others. 'Sorry,' he smiled down at her, 'don't think I'm always this rude, but we haven't much time . . . it's about you and Terry.'

'Yes?' Sheelagh felt herself stiffen, every nerve alert, as she stared back up into the captain's face with wide eyes.

'He sends you his love and good wishes,' Johns said softly, his iron-grey eyes holding Sheelagh's gaze steadily, 'and he says he thinks you'll understand why he isn't here personally to give them to you. However,' the pilot went on before Sheelagh could so much as think of any sort of a reply, 'he wants me to give you this,' he dived a hand into the side-pocket of his uniform and pulled out a small, gift-wrapped package.

'It's from all of us, perhaps I should add,' he smiled as he pressed the square-shaped package into Sheelagh's hand, 'from the whole team. Now you'd better get back to your friends . . . and this is on behalf of the team, too.'

Before she knew what was happening, Sheelagh felt his lips touch her cheek in a brief kiss. And then he was gone, waving cheerily to her little group, striding away through the crowds towards the entrance foyer.

Sheelagh waved down from the window of the plane as the engines began to splutter into life, thinking what a handsome pair Aileen and Louis made, crying silently as she returned Mrs Newman's hastily thrown kiss. And then they were rolling forward across the concrete apron of the airfield and her three friends had disappeared, had merged into the dark mass of the crowd pressed against the wire fencing farewelling the aircraft.

As per schedule, they touched down at Chicago, then flew directly on to San Francisco. For Sheelagh, it was the shortest, quickest trip of her life, because for most of it she had simply sat staring out of the cabin window at the cloud patterns above which they flew. In her lap was the gift that Captain Harry Johns, on behalf of his crew, had presented her with, and the gift-paper in which it still nestled was damp from Sheelagh's tears.

It was one of those carefully thought out presents that always mean so much more than the more conventional and habitual gifts. It was a tiny gold-plated model of a Boeing 707, the type of aircraft they had worked on together, and on the small metal plate that formed the base were inscribed the words:

To Sheelagh, the best jet nurse in the business. From the Gang of H-52.

Sheelagh rubbed her forefinger across the inscription with loving care as their aircraft began its wide, gentle descent, wondering—even as she unconsciously admired the sheer beauty of San Francisco Bay—how many times she had scribbled down that combination of letters and numerals—H-52—that had been the code designation of their plane.

She looked at the familiar and beloved city as their altitude dropped. The graceful span of the Golden Gate Bridge, the clutter of colour that was Telegraph Hill, the dark green splotches that were the famous 'Frisco parks—Buena Vista, Golden Gate Park, the Zoo. Then almost before Sheelagh knew it there came the vague thumping noise of the tricycle landing gear extending down beneath the aircraft and locking into position, followed almost immediately by the shrill hydraulic whine as the brake flaps were extended from the trailing edges of the wings. Then came the final screech and thump that told of a perfect landing, and they were idling across the concrete towards the terminal building and, Sheelagh hoped and prayed, Dr Michael Kelman.

He wasn't there! That was the first and only

thought Sheelagh was aware of as she hurried down the ramp, joined the line of passengers moving towards the small, scattered crowd of people waiting to welcome the travellers.

Fitzy was there, as plump as ever, waving her gloves to attract Sheelagh's attention and jumping up and down in her excitement, but there was no sign of Michael.

'Honey! Gee, but it's good to see you!'

Fitzy grabbed Sheelagh in a bear-hug when she was finally free of the formalities, had been allowed through and into the terminus proper, nearly knocking Sheelagh off her feet so great was her enthusiasm.

'Hullo, Fitzy!' Sheelagh smiled, her eyes flicking every which way, trying to spot Michael's familiar figure among the men gathered throughout the area. 'It's mighty good to see you, too, and thanks a million for coming all this way out to meet me.'

'Now just who do you think you're kidding, honey?' Fitzy asked, stepping back a few paces and looking Sheelagh over, a head-to-toe-and-back-again examination, as though to check on what sort of condition her friend had returned in. '*I'm* not the one you want to see, any more than you want to find Anne Northrupp, or Judy or Thelma, or any of the other girls waiting for your plane. And incidentally,' she added quickly before Sheelagh could begin to protest, 'they all of them, especially Anne, send their love and regrets. It just worked out I was the only one free from duty when the airline people decided to schedule this Washington–Chicago–San Francisco flight.'

'And ... and Michael?' Sheelagh could not pretend any longer. She had to know!

'Cursing whichever particular demon takes care of Irishmen, I shouldn't wonder. You just wouldn't read about it! He and I were all organised to come out and meet you when some character decided to take a tumble through a plateglass window. Emergency buzzed for Mike, and right now I guess he's wondering just how to sew back on this particular patient's left foot. Ugh!' Fitzy made a face and raised her eyes to the sky. 'You never *saw* such a mess. When some members of this general public we're devoted to serving decide to cut themselves up they really do the thing properly.'

'Then,' Sheelagh felt her face flush a deep red, 'then he's all right? I mean, everything's okay?'

'He's been counting the days, then the hours, now I guess he's down to the minutes, to see you,' Fitzy grinned. 'I think that little flying vacation you decided to take worked something of a miracle. Did Terry tell you how miserable your man's been?'

Sheelagh nodded silently, remembering the last, the final scene with Terry. Fitzy chattered on:

'It's true! Everyone's been talking about it. Talk about a bear with a sore head—heck, you just couldn't *look* at that man of yours. Now I'm not a gambling woman, but I'm prepared to lay my next month's pay that the first thing he asks you to do is marry him ... and I don't care *what* kind of good and fatherly advice Wilky and Dr Kerensky have been pumping into him about staying in the single state until he's a top-class surgeon!'

Sheelagh barely caught the last few words, she was hurrying towards the exit. If the mountain wouldn't—or in this case, couldn't—come to its Mohammed, then she, Nurse Mohammed Sheelagh Landers, would surely go to her mountain.

He was still wearing his tight surgeon's cap, and the front of his theatre scrub-suit was slightly stained with the blood of his patient. He was walking slowly away from the theatre's sub-sterilising room, and Sheelagh barely recognised him. His shoulders were bowed, and his walk was the gait of a tired old man. Dark circles surrounded his eyes, and the corners of his mouth dropped dejectedly.

'Darling! Michael!'

She ran the rest of the way, hurling herself into his arms, not caring that his clothes were what in hospital language were known as 'dirty', or that he smelt of anaesthetic, carried the atmosphere of the operating theatre with him, in fact. She cared only that his arms circled her automatically, that they tightened until she thought her chest would be crushed, and that his face lit up as though by a miracle as he cried out her name.

Neither of them spoke for a long time after that, for it is impossible to utter so much as a single syllable when two people who have not seen one another for months and who love one another deeply finally meet up. For them another language is used, a language understood only by lovers.

His lips were fierce and demanding, and he seemed oblivious to the fact that people were coming and going along the corridor, that nurses were tittering, that other doctors were either laughing or coughing in sudden embarrassment.

'Michael . . . please!' Sheelagh finally managed to come up for air, pulling her face down from his mouth, pressing her cheek against the coolness of his scrub-suit.

'Marry me?' he said by way of reply, slipping a strong finger beneath Sheelagh's chin and forcefully chucking her head back and up so that they gazed into one another's eyes. 'It's the thing I've been promising myself I'd say the very moment I saw you, and if you dare to say no back to the jets you go!'

'It looks like I owe Fitzy a month's pay,' Sheelagh laughed, 'or are you two in on this deal together?'

'I don't know what the hell you're talking about,' he grinned, brushing his lips down the side of Sheelagh's face, lightly kissing her neck, then moving his mouth back as he began kissing her ear, his teeth nibbling gently at the lobe. He went on, 'And I don't particularly care . . . all I want to hear you say is yes.'

'Yes!' Sheelagh whispered obediently, closing her eyes, thrilling to the wonderful excitement of the moment, pressing herself tightly against him, loving the closeness of his embrace.

'That's my girl!' he chuckled, moving back to look at her, then slowly coming in once again, his lips already eager for the kiss. 'No more jet nursing for you . . . from now on consider yourself the future wife of Dr Michael Kelman. Okay?'

'Okay!' Sheelagh just managed to get out before his mouth covered her own. And then, once again, they were back to speaking the language of lovers that is as old and as wonderful as time itself.

Doctor Nurse Romances

Don't miss
July's
other story of love and romance amid the pressure
and emotion of medical life.

OMEN FOR LOVE
by Esther Boyd

When Nurse Carol Baxter decided that she was tired of
taking orders from her stuffy fiancé, she left him to
join Dr Ian Morrison's immunisation programme in the
jungles of Peru — and found herself at the beck and
call of another dictator! Was it only a coincidence that
the flower Ian gave her was regarded as a bad omen in
Peru?

Masquerade
Historical Romances

*Intrigue
excitement
romance*

COUNT ANTONOV'S HEIR
by Christina Laffeaty

To Caroline Kearley, fresh from England, Imperial
Russia was a bewildering place where magnificence
and privilege existed side by side with poverty and
degradation. And she held a secret that could strip
Count Alexander Antonov — whom she loved more
than her own happiness — of his wealth and power
overnight!

CAPTAIN BLACK
by Caroline Martin

Wealthy Puritan heiress Deborah Halsey was kidnapped
so that her ransom could swell the Royalist coffers —
and to strike a blow at Sir Edward Biddulph, her
betrothed. The man who captured her was Sir
Edward's mortal enemy — so why should Deborah
feel so happy as prisoner of the notorious Captain
Black?

Look out for these titles in your local paperback shop from
11th July 1980

Doctor Nurse Romances

Have you enjoyed these recent titles in our
Doctor Nurse series?

STAFF NURSE AT ST. MILDRED'S
by Janet Ferguson

Staff Nurse Jill Thompson was not used to feeling
unsure of herself. She liked things to be well organised,
like her future with Clive Farmer. But perhaps she was
only clinging to Clive because Dr Guy Ferring, her
boss at St. Mildred's, disturbed her so . . .

THE RUSTLE OF BAMBOO
by Celine Conway

Inexperienced as she was, Nurse Pat Millay found it
hard going at the little hospital on the Burmese island
of Pelonga. And that was before she had experienced
the abrasive effect of Dr Mark Bradlaw's personality
— or fallen in love with him . . .